J
92
O'Donnell

Y0-BDU-505

Rosie O'Donnell

60901 – April 2000

Lucent Books, San Diego, CA

Titles in the People in the News series include:

Jim Carrey
Bill Gates
John Grisham
Michael Jordan
Stephen King
Dominique Moceanu
Rosie O'Donnell
The Rolling Stones
Steven Spielberg
Oprah Winfrey
Tiger Woods

PEOPLE
IN THE NEWS

Rosie O'Donnell

by Stuart A. Kallen

Lucent Books, San Diego, CA

No part of this book may be reproduced or used in any form or by any means, electrical, mechanical, or otherwise, including, but not limited to, photocopy, recording, or any information storage and retrieval system, without prior written permission from the publisher.

Library of Congress Cataloging-in-Publication Data

Kallen, Stuart A., 1955–
    Rosie O'Donnell / by Stuart A. Kallen.
      p. cm. — (People in the news)
    Includes bibliographical references and index.
    Summary: Follows the life and career of popular comedienne Rosie O'Donnell.
    ISBN 1-56006-546-X (lib. : alk. paper)
    1. O'Donnell, Rosie—Juvenile literature. 2. Comedians—United States—Biography—Juvenile literature. 3. Motion picture actors and actresses—United States—Biography—Juvenile literature. 4. Television personalities—United States—Biography—Juvenile literature. [1. O'Donnell, Rosie. 2. Comedians. 3. Entertainers. 4. Women—Biography.] I. Title. II. Series.
PN2287.027K36   1999
792.7'028'092—dc21
                                                                                 98-52126
                                                                                    CIP
                                                                                     AC

[b]   **3 5944 00060 9014**

Copyright © 1999 by Lucent Books, Inc.
P.O. Box 289011
San Diego, CA 92198-9011
Printed in the U.S.A.

Table of Contents

Foreword

FAME AND CELEBRITY are alluring. People are drawn to those who walk in fame's spotlight, whether they are known for great accomplishments or for notorious deeds. The lives of the famous pique public interest and attract attention, perhaps because their experiences seem in some ways so different from, yet in other ways so similar to, our own.

Newspapers, magazines, and television regularly capitalize on this fascination with celebrity by running profiles of famous people. For example, television programs such as *Entertainment Tonight* devote all of their programming to stories about entertainment and entertainers. Magazines such as *People* fill their pages with stories of the private lives of famous people. Even newspapers, newsmagazines, and television news frequently delve into the lives of well-known personalities. Despite the number of articles and programs, few provide more than a superficial glimpse at their subjects.

Lucent's People in the News series offers young readers a deeper look into the lives of today's newsmakers, the influences that have shaped them, and the impact they have had in their fields of endeavor and on other people's lives. The subjects of the series hail from many disciplines and walks of life. They include authors, musicians, athletes, political leaders, entertainers, entrepreneurs, and others who have made a mark on modern life and who, in many cases, will continue to do so for years to come.

These biographies are more than factual chronicles. Each book emphasizes the contributions, accomplishments, or deeds that have brought fame or notoriety to the individual and shows how that person has influenced modern life. Authors portray their subjects in a realistic, unsentimental light. For example, Bill Gates—the cofounder and chief executive officer of the software giant Microsoft—has been instrumental in making personal computers the most vital tool of the modern age. Few dispute his business savvy, his perseverance, or his technical expertise, yet critics say he is ruthless in his dealings with competitors and driven more by his desire to maintain Microsoft's dominance in the computer industry than by an interest in furthering technology.

In these books, young readers will encounter inspiring stories about real people who achieved success despite enormous obstacles. Oprah Winfrey—the most powerful, most watched, and wealthiest woman on television today—spent the first six years of her life in the care of her grandparents while her unwed mother sought work and a better life elsewhere. Her adolescence was colored by promiscuity, pregnancy at age fourteen, rape, and sexual abuse.

Each author documents and supports his or her work with an array of primary and secondary source quotations taken from diaries, letters, speeches, and interviews. All quotes are footnoted to show readers exactly how and where biographers derive their information and provide guidance for further research. The quotations enliven the text by giving readers eyewitness views of the life and accomplishments of each person covered in the People in the News series.

In addition, each book in the series includes photographs, annotated bibliographies, timelines, and comprehensive indexes. For both the casual reader and the student researcher, the People in the News series offers insight into the lives of today's newsmakers—people who shape the way we live, work, and play in the modern age.

A Fairy Tale Come True

Some say Rosie O'Donnell's life is a fairy tale come true. She started out working in comedy clubs at the age of sixteen. This led to a highly successful career as a stand-up comedian. Next, she became a movie star after appearing in *A League of Their Own* with actress Geena Davis and superstar Madonna. After appearing in several successful movies, O'Donnell got her own television show, which quickly became the top-rated talk show in the country. In show business circles, Rosie O'Donnell's name was now mentioned in the same breath as the highly successful Oprah Winfrey as the queen of daytime TV.

But Rosie O'Donnell's success did not come easily. She suffered a major childhood trauma when her mother died. She had to overcome sexism in the comedy world as one of the few female stand-up comedians in the early 1980s. And she had her share of rejections and setbacks as she tried to climb the ladder to success.

What appeared to be "overnight success" was actually eighteen years of hard work in an often unforgiving world of show business. Along the way, critics panned O'Donnell for her weight, her Long Island accent, and her unconventional personality. Despite the criticisms, O'Donnell knew, since she was eight years old, that she would be famous, and she believed in herself enough to pursue her dream.

Using Celebrity to Help Others

Rosie O'Donnell grew rich and famous because of her talents. But many think that it is more than her talent that got her where she is today. O'Donnell's personality goes beyond her sense of humor, friendly smile, and charming manner. Although she

8

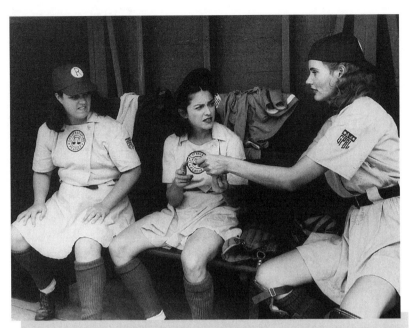

(Left to right) Doris (Rosie), Mae (Madonna), and Dottie (Geena Davis) discuss strategy in Columbia Pictures' A League of Their Own.

grew up as a streetwise kid not far from New York City, friends and fans alike portray Rosie O'Donnell as a truly nice human being who cares about others.

Many people who earn tens of millions of dollars in show business spend their time shopping, traveling, and living a life of luxury. But that life is not what O'Donnell wants. Instead, she travels the country raising millions of dollars for charities that help children, women, and people who have incurable diseases.

The life story of Rosie O'Donnell contains lessons for many people. Although O'Donnell downplays the example she sets, she has become a role model for children. And her generous ways set examples for adults as well. Some fans see her as the big sister they never had or as a rowdy best friend with a heart of gold. But O'Donnell is a woman who rose above difficult circumstances, who used humor to ease her pain, and who, when she made it big, used her celebrity to help others who needed it the most.

Chapter 1

Growing Up Roseann

LONG ISLAND LIES to the east of New York City, stretching out into the Atlantic Ocean for 120 miles. The island is packed with miles of suburban housing developments, but it is also home to "the Hamptons," the swank summer resort for the rich and famous. Nowhere on the island is farther than four hours from midtown Manhattan, where the bright lights of Broadway serve as a beacon to thousands of hopeful actors, actresses, singers, dancers, and comedians.

Long Island is home to more than 2.8 million Americans and has long been a favored settling ground for people emigrating from Ireland. In the 1960s, Edward J. O'Donnell, thirty-four, was one of those Irish immigrants who had settled on Long Island. His wife, American born, but also 100 percent Irish, was Roseann O'Donnell. The couple lived in a two-story, brick-and-cedar-shake house on 17 Rhonda Lane in Commack, a typical middle-class suburban community. Rosie O'Donnell's description of her hometown appears in George Mair and Anna Green's 1997 book *Rosie O'Donnell: Her True Story:* "tract row houses one after another, exactly the same. Different colored shutters were the only way you could tell them apart."[1]

Although O'Donnell has described her neighborhood as "suburban hell," it was not as grim as she made it out to be. The street where she lived was lined with large oaks and maples. The houses sat back off the street surrounded by large lawns and ample backyards. The young Rosie and her friends enjoyed a nearby one-hundred-acre park called Hoyt Farm that contained playground equipment and a "petting zoo" with baby farm animals. On Sunday evenings in the summer, people would go to the park to enjoy live bands and family picnics. A former classmate remembers Rosie's neighborhood as a great place to grow up. "We all used to leave our doors unlocked, we walked to the buses by ourselves. It was the kind of town . . . where the grandparents lived with the families."[2]

The O'Donnell Family

After the O'Donnells were married they quickly started a family. Their first child, Edward Jr., was born in 1960. He was followed by Daniel in 1961. Then on March 21, 1962, the O'Donnells had their first girl, whom they named after Mrs. O'Donnell. Little Roseann (no middle name) was only fifteen months old when her sister, Maureen, was born. The final O'Donnell child, Timothy, was born in 1966. Roseann's little brother could not say her name properly, so he called her Dolly. Until she was twelve, Roseann's entire family called her by that nickname.

It was a short drive to the Fairchild Corporation where Edward O'Donnell was employed as an electrical engineer. His job at the company involved designing top-secret cameras for satellites made for the U.S. government. Although Edward's job met the family's basic needs, it was a financial burden to feed and clothe seven people. Rosie remembers the family making many small sacrifices. "We didn't really have many luxuries when we were children. We didn't have matching socks. Or top sheets for the bed, just the bottom sheet."[3]

Rosie O'Donnell elaborated on her family's financial situation in a June 1997 interview with Liz Smith in *Good Housekeeping* magazine:

> We weren't poor—my father was an electrical engineer. But there were five children. The kids who went to school with us in Dix Hills [NY] would all get Camaros on their six-teenth birthdays. And at our house, we had a Plymouth Volare with an AM radio. All five of us kids had to use that car. We went to the flea market to buy clothes, not Macy's.[4]

As with most other families in the 1960s, Roseann's mother did not have a job outside the home. Mrs. O'Donnell took time to serve as president of the PTA, where she was well liked because of the jokes she told. Rosie told *Good Housekeeping:*

I remember that she was funny. I remember her coming to my elementary school—she was in the PTA—and all the teachers would go out of the room to talk to her. They'd say to us, "Read your books. We'll be right back." There were glass windows along the hallway, and I remember watching my mom making all the teachers laugh. Once, I went to a PTA meeting with her, and she went up to speak and had everyone laughing. I remember feeling like that was an amazing thing, and wanting to be like her in that way.[5]

Mrs. O'Donnell has been described as a dark-haired, blue-eyed beauty who bore a resemblance to the young actress Elizabeth Taylor. Roseann looked like her mom and she also shared her sense of humor. "I knew she had this thing people wanted—that people would go to her because of this comedy thing."[6]

Roseann's father was the opposite of her mother—quiet and serious. Although she described him in interviews as "the Lucky Charms elf," he was a close-mouthed man, a hard drinker, stern, with ultraconservative political views. Rosie has said that Edward, an engineer, was "emotionally unavailable" for the kids. He spoke with a heavy Irish accent, known as a brogue, which O'Donnell later imitated in her stand-up routines.

A Love for Theater and TV

Roseann's childhood was shaped by her neighborhood, which was full of large Irish and Italian families. There were plenty of kids around to play games, and Roseann was always eager to participate. "I was a tomboy—is that a shock to anyone? I didn't do ballet. I played softball, volleyball, kickball, tennis, and basketball; a regular tomboy jock girl and proud of it."[7] But when O'Donnell looks back at her young life, her favorite memories are not of sports or games, but of traveling on the Long Island Railroad into Manhattan with her mother. There mother and daughter would head for a lavish stage and film show at Radio City Music Hall. The O'Donnells could only afford the cheaper seats in the third balcony, but the two Roseanns eagerly watched the show and shared a giant box of lemon drop candies

Rosie's favorite childhood memories were of trips with her mother to shows at Manhattan's Radio City Music Hall.

purchased in the lobby. Mrs. O'Donnell loved theater so much that she arranged the family's schedule around the next Barbra Streisand TV special. The household budget included money for the purchase of cast albums from Broadway plays.

The television was on constantly in the O'Donnell home. Rosie later told an interviewer:

> My whole family knew the entire fall [television] schedule before it even went on the air. We had the *Newsday* [magazine] supplement and we'd memorize what was on. We were a huge, huge, huge TV family.[8]

Roseann grew up on a steady diet of TV sitcoms (situation comedies) such as *Gilligan's Island, I Dream of Jeannie,* and *Bewitched.* She also drew inspiration from variety shows hosted by Ed Sullivan, Jackie Gleason, and Red Skelton. These shows exposed the young Roseann to every manner of entertainment

Multitalented Carol Burnett (center) was Rosie's childhood idol.

from dancing poodles to the Beatles. Most of all, Roseann admired Carol Burnett, who could sing, dance, act, and tell jokes. The little girl wanted to grow up to be just like her.

Family Tragedy

In 1972, when Roseann was ten years old, Mrs. O'Donnell, thirty-six, was diagnosed with pancreatic and liver cancer, and was told she had only had a few months to live. Their mother's illness was confusing for the five O'Donnell children.

> They told us at first she had hepatitis. They thought that was a big word and kids wouldn't know. But I went to the library and looked it up, and it said it was a disease that you got from dirty needles. I thought to myself it was from sewing. That's the kind of household it was—you had to draw your own conclusions, because you weren't really allowed to ask.[9]

Roseann O'Donnell died on St. Patrick's Day (March 17), 1973, four days before Roseann's eleventh birthday. She was told her mother had "passed away" but was not allowed to attend the funeral. Young Roseann didn't even understand what the phrase meant and sometimes wondered if her mother had simply moved away because it was too much work raising five children. "Being a typically repressed and emotionally detached Irish Catholic family, we rarely discussed my mother's death,"[10] she told Patrick Pacheco, in a June 1994 interview in *Cosmopolitan.*

The death of her mother caused Roseann serious emotional trauma, perhaps because of the silence surrounding it. O'Donnell told Melina Gerosa in a February 1997 article in *Ladies' Home Journal:*

[My mother's death] wasn't spoken about in our house. All of my mother's things were removed. When my father

The Budding Entertainer

Rosie O'Donnell's mother always made sure she purchased the original cast album of a Broadway play. Roseann memorized these albums and can still recall the words to songs from *South Pacific, Oklahoma, The Sound of Music,* and *Mary Poppins.*

As the middle child, the young Roseann grabbed the family's attention imitating what she saw on the stage and screen. And Roseann wanted to be a performer from the time she was in kindergarten. In 1997 in an article for *Ladies' Home Journal,* she told interviewer Melina Gerosa:

For show-and-tell, kids are bringing in Barbie dolls, and I'm singing "Oklahoma." In 1973 I saw Bette Midler on Broadway, and I thought, "That's what I want to do." I'd watch Barbra Streisand and think, I want to be her. Carol Burnett, Lucille Ball—I wanted to be the funny women, and when I saw characters like Ethel (Mertz on *The Lucy Show*) and Rhoda (Morgenstern on *The Mary Tyler Moore Show*), I [said], "Now there's a role for me."

Roseann's acting debut came in the third grade, when she played Glinda the Good Witch in *The Wizard of Oz.*

removed my mother's things, her records were the one thing that he left. So [Barbra] Streisand [records were] a connection to my mom.[11]

Because O'Donnell was so young, she barely has memories of her mother. She told Kristen Golden in an interview in the January/February 1997 issue of *Ms.* magazine, "I have some sense memories; I remember the smell of her perfume. My memories are through a child's mind."[12] (Today, O'Donnell gets a lot of letters from children whose mothers have died. She responds by telling them to keep their memories of their mothers alive by talking with family members and by writing down whatever they recall.)

"My whole life revolves around my mother's death," O'Donnell told *Ladies' Home Journal* twenty-five years later. "It changed who I am as a person. I don't know who I would be if my mother would have lived. But I would trade it all in to see."[13] The death of O'Donnell's mother gave Rosie a strong incentive to set goals and work to obtain them. "I remember thinking at ten years old, if I was going to die in my thirties, what would I want to have achieved? It made me strive for my goals with a fervent passion."[14]

Rosie refused to acknowledge her mother's death for many years.

People would call and ask, "Is your mother home?" And I would say, "She's in the shower, can you call back?" And one day my college roommate asked, "Why do you always talk about your father, and never your mother?" I stopped for a moment, and I remember having to choke the words out: "Well, she died." That was the first time I ever said it.[15]

Relying on Television and Each Other

After her mother's death, Roseann's father became even more emotionally remote. He spent his weekends drinking and playing the sentimental records of an Irish singing group called the Clancy Brothers.

The children were left to look after themselves. O'Donnell admits that they grew up wild, with no discipline and little respect for authority. With no adult at home to act as a parent while their father worked, the O'Donnell siblings miraculously maintained a household all by themselves. Their mother had prepared them to some extent: Each child knew the recipe for cooking one meal, and each would take turns preparing his or her specialty.

In a role reversal, Roseann's oldest brother, Eddie, did much of the cleaning; Roseann assigned chores, refereed fights, and got in scrapes at school protecting her siblings. Roseann, in effect, became the mother *and* father of her brothers and sister.

O'Donnell relied on a steady stream of TV shows like *Eight Is Enough, The Brady Bunch,* and *The Partridge Family* to fill the void left by her mother's death. She told Melina Gerosa: "I would watch these shows hoping that my father would meet a [woman like those on TV] who would bring love and life back to our home." [16]

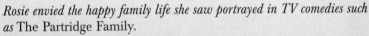

Rosie envied the happy family life she saw portrayed in TV comedies such as The Partridge Family.

In an interview with Liz Smith, O'Donnell recalled:

> My whole family became fixated on TV. I think it was
> some sort of surrogate parenting. I wanted *Eight Is
> Enough* to happen to my family, you know? I wanted
> Abby—or some widow—to come and be my mom. I
> lived all my emotional life through movies or TV. I
> would see a movie and cry and cry, but not about my
> own loss or pain—about what was happening in the
> movie. That's the way it is to this day.[17]

O'Donnell relied on her sense of humor to help her cope with
the loss of her mother. "After our mother died, if you wanted to
express something painful, you could only do it couched in comedy,"[18] she explained.

Learning from the Best

Edward O'Donnell's alcoholism offered Roseann one opportunity to feed her love for the theater. The morning after his drinking bouts, while her father was safely passed out in the living
room, the teenage Roseann would pick his pocket. She would
take enough money to hop the Long Island Railroad into
Manhattan and pay for an inexpensive standing-room ticket to a
matinee performance of a Broadway show.

Roseann's bedroom became a shrine to her love of show
business. Every inch of every wall of her bedroom was covered
with Bette Midler and Barbra Streisand posters. Every day she
practiced becoming like her heroines, standing in front of a mir-
ror singing into a wooden kitchen spoon, pretending it was a microphone. She recalled:

> I was kind of an unhappy kid . . . looking for dreams to
> give me solace . . . and my dreams of [Midler and
> Streisand] . . . performing and what I perceived their
> lives to be gave me such comfort.[19]

As she grew older, O'Donnell ventured out to more and
more concerts, plays, and films. She was obsessed with movies
and would often go to them alone, sometimes seeing two or

For Bette Midler Rosie was "the fan from hell."

three in one day. She kept large scrapbooks filled with ticket stubs, programs, fan magazines, autographs, and newspaper ads.

In 1975, the groundbreaking comedy show *Saturday Night Live* debuted on NBC. O'Donnell quickly became a fan of the

Rosie's Obsession with Bette Midler

Rosie O'Donnell has always been obsessed with Bette Midler. O'Donnell wrote an article for *McCall's* in May 1997 about her love of Midler.

> Bette Midler is the reason I'm in entertainment today. I owe her my life! I was 12 years old when I saw her on Broadway in *Clams on the Half Shell*. I stole ten dollars out of my father's wallet to buy a ticket. . . .
>
> Over the years, I kept a Bette scrapbook—and I still have it. I have every album she's ever made; I know every lyric to every song by heart. . . .
>
> In 1984, when I was a stand-up comic, I called her fan club and got her . . . concert schedule. I booked myself in the same cities where she was appearing, and then I called in sick at comedy clubs so I could go see her. I saw her 26 times.
>
> So given all this obsession, you can imagine how terrified I was the first time Bette and I met. It was several years ago—I was going to the wedding of one of her . . . backup singers . . . with a friend. . . . The three of us rode together in a limo. I felt absolutely sick to my stomach (because of nerves). There she was! The Queen of All Things! Her Highness! My Idol! Bette now says this was the longest limo ride of her life because I wouldn't shut up, or stop singing. It was her biggest nightmare: being trapped with the fan from hell.

show and learned to imitate the distinctive characters that were a hallmark of the early years of the show. When she was in seventh grade, she curled her long, dark hair into a perm. Because of her first name O'Donnell instantly became known among her friends as Roseanne Roseannadanna—a Gilda Radner character from *Saturday Night Live*. "That's how I started doing comedy. I'd do Gilda Radner impressions,"[20] O'Donnell said.

Once O'Donnell got her driver's license, she was able to stay out later, pursuing her obsession. One of her favorite sports was stalking singer and fellow Long Islander Billy Joel, who was just achieving major success at that time. O'Donnell would take the family station wagon and track Joel to bars and nightclubs. Once she spotted him, she would call all her friends, and they would descend on the singer, seeking autographs or just making conversation.

"Little Miss Overachiever"

Roseann didn't rebel in traditional teenage ways—she didn't smoke or use drugs. She did cause her father to be worried, though. Her show-business obsession led her to stay out late at night and skip school in order to see plays and movies. But O'Donnell ignored her father's warnings against the fickle nature of show business. She just *knew* she would be successful. As she told *Cosmopolitan* magazine in 1994: "I got away with that attitude because I was funny. I was lucky I wasn't prone to getting into trouble. I was a kid prone to succeed."[21]

In spite of her outside activities O'Donnell maintained a B average at Commack High School, where she herself says she

Rosie started in comedy by imitating Gilda Radner's character, Roseanne Roseannadanna.

was "Little Miss Overachiever." O'Donnell's sense of humor, combined with her readiness for adventure and her energizing personality, made her terrifically popular. She was a member of the student council, senior class president, and played in every sport at school. As a pretty young girl with a wholesome Irish beauty, O'Donnell was also chosen for the ultimate high school honors—on separate occasions she was voted as Homecoming Queen and Prom Queen. Along the way she was also voted Most School Spirited, Class Clown, and Personality Plus. In short, O'Donnell became the life of every party.

Even O'Donnell's friends believed she would achieve her dreams of stardom. According to the James Robert Parish book, *Rosie:*

> Everybody knew what I was going to do. On the year-book they'd write: "Say hello to [former talk-show host] Johnny Carson when you're a big star." [22]

What they didn't know is just how big a star their high school friend was destined to become.

Chapter 2

Playing the Comedy Clubs

Rosie O'Donnell made her stand-up comedy debut at the age of sixteen at a local restaurant called the Ground Round. It was open mike (microphone) night, which was a time when any amateur could get on stage and try out three minutes of material on a live audience. O'Donnell later recalled her moment in the spotlight in George Mair and Anna Green's book, *Rosie O'Donnell: Her True Story:*

> I had no act at all. When you're sixteen you haven't lived enough to have any observations. So I hid behind a pair of goofy glasses, pointed at guys in the audience, and said things like, "Hey Buddy, where'd you get that shirt—K-Mart blue light special?" When you're sixteen you're so cocky, even when I bombed it was exciting.

> I was sixteen but I looked twelve, with this cute little haircut and big sweatshirt and sweatpants, and I was this tough little girl. The audience—grown-ups my father's age—were like, "Look at this little kid with *chutzpah* (nerve)." I was fearless.[23]

Onto the Comedy Stage

In O'Donnell's last year at Commack High School, she performed her Gilda Radner impression at the Senior Follies. A man in the audience heard O'Donnell and invited her to perform at his comedy club. This was a step up from the open mike—she would be paid to perform for an audience. Since she had no material, she rushed home from school the next day to watch a popular daytime talk show called *The Mike Douglas Show*. As luck would have it, a funny new comic performed on the program that day. O'Donnell wrote down every joke the comedian told.

That night the seventeen-year-old got on stage at a real comedy club and was a smash hit. People were howling with laughter. But O'Donnell's spirits fell back to earth with a thud when she left the stage and was suddenly surrounded by a mob of angry comics.

> "You can't do that! Where'd you get those jokes?" they demanded. And I said, "Jerry Sein-man or something." And I was so mad, because I thought, why do I have to write the jokes *and* do them? It's so unfair. I thought once a guy does his jokes on TV you were allowed to use them. I thought a joke was a joke, like Bazooka Joe— you open it up and there's a joke. It never occurred to me that I was stealing.[24]

It turned out that O'Donnell had lifted the routine of a budding young comic named Jerry Seinfeld. And she not only took his jokes, but she stole his vocal cadence and his timing as well. O'Donnell felt that since an actress isn't expected to *write* the movie she's starring in, then a comedian shouldn't have to write comedy.

On the way home from the club O'Donnell became depressed and felt like giving up. She didn't think she could ever pull jokes out of thin air. But the laughter and applause were addictive, so she decided to try another route to stardom. She became an emcee, introducing performers at the many comedy venues that were popping up in Long Island at that time.

O'Donnell could watch experienced comedians perform their routines while being paid fifteen dollars a night as an emcee. Instead of writing her own "bits" she turned to the type of insult comedy made famous by Don Rickles—mocking people's haircuts and clothes. Many years later, in an interview in *Good Housekeeping* magazine, O'Donnell related what got her through those early years on stage.

In a stand-up performance when she was 17, Rosie stole Jerry Seinfeld's entire routine and was a big success.

It was hard, for many, many years. It took guts. But I was 17 when I started, and because of that I had a very big ego. When people didn't laugh, I thought they were stupid. My adolescent arrogance carried me right through. I had that "try anything" attitude. But I had to learn how to be funny onstage. So when my friends were at the prom or out partying, I'd be sitting in the back at the East Side Comedy Club, taking notes, trying to see how the comics formed a joke, how they made a segue.[25]

Hits and Misses

Before long, O'Donnell's scrutiny of local comics led her to develop an observational comedy routine of her own. (Observational comedy is a routine in which a comic takes a typical life experience and puts humor into it. If the jokes work as intended, the audience laughs at the comedy because they too have experienced that situation.) Once she had developed her own routine, O'Donnell began to spend her nights zigzagging across Long Island for any chance to get onstage.

Meanwhile, her father was pushing her to attend college so she would have a career to fall back on if she was to fail in show business. O'Donnell spent her freshman year on scholarship at Dickinson College in Carlisle, Pennsylvania, where she worked at the school post office in a work-study job. O'Donnell felt that she didn't fit in: As she put it, Dickinson was a school for "people much smarter than me."[26] Her opinion seemed confirmed when O'Donnell only achieved a D-minus average—not good enough to continue at Dickinson.

The next year O'Donnell transferred to Boston University, where she enrolled in the theater program. Her time as a college student ended about six months later, when her drama professor criticized her in class. He told her the part of Rhoda Morgenstern (Mary's best friend on *The Mary Tyler Moore Show*) was already taken, so O'Donnell would never make it as an actress.

O'Donnell's response to her professor's harsh words was to drop out of college. But the criticism also hardened her resolve to succeed as a comedian. And she was in the right place to do it. At the time, Boston was a comedy club boomtown, and in 1982, O'Donnell got her first paid job as a professional comic. Like her comedy debut a few years earlier, it was almost a disaster.

O'Donnell bluffed her way into Boston's Comedy Connection by telling the doorman that she was an experienced New York comic. That ploy worked, but then the manager approached O'Donnell and told her one of the comics at another club run by the Comedy Connection in Worcester had not shown up. The manager of the club recalls what happened next in *Rosie O'Donnell: Her True Story:*

> There was a car leaving right then, so without seeing her act, they put her in a car with [comedians] Denis Leary and Steven Wright and sent them off on an hour and a half drive to a club called Plums in Worcester. She didn't fare too well, but they paid her anyway. There were no hard feelings. The manager from Plums called and said "Oh my God—nice girl," but she definitely didn't have it.[27]

After the show, when all the comedians autographed their photos to hang on the wall of the club, O'Donnell wrote: "Thanks for my first sixty bucks." (Several years later O'Donnell and Leary would win comedy awards in Las Vegas for best female and male comic. It would be the first time they had seen each other since the Plums show in Worcester.)

After a few months, O'Donnell drifted back to Long Island, where she landed the only desk job she ever had—working in the catalog department at Sears.

Learning Improv Comedy

Comedy that is made up on the spot by comics using suggestions from the audience is called improvisational comedy, or improv. When O'Donnell found herself back in Long Island she auditioned for an improv troupe called the Laughter Company. O'Donnell beat out sixty-five other hopefuls to land a spot in the improv company.

Rosie began her career competing for laughs against established stand-ups such as Denis Leary.

Roseann Becomes Rosie

Until she was twenty, everyone called Rosie O'Donnell "Roseann." In 1982, an emcee at a comedy club introduced the comedian as Roseann O'Donnell. The audience misunderstood and thought they were about to see Gilda Radner performing Roseanne Roseannadanna, her popular character from *Saturday Night Live*. When O'Donnell appeared on stage, the audience started booing. The next time she was introduced, the emcee dubbed O'Donnell "Rosie," and she's been known by that name ever since.

The Laughter Company found popularity very quickly and attracted a loyal following for their two-hour shows on Monday nights at a club called the Eastside Comedy Club. They performed comedy skits that they had rehearsed, and they also improvised using ideas shouted out to them by members of the audience. It was fast-paced, frenzied comedy that provided excellent training for the performers in that it forced them to think on their feet.

O'Donnell was the youngest member of the troupe, lively and trim, with a shag haircut and a dynamic manner. O'Donnell played various roles in short skits, from a police officer to an Irish nun. The troupe ended their shows with sword fights using imaginary weapons and improvised sound effects. The stage lights would go down to darkness and an actor would say, "You have just been victims of the Laughter Company."[28]

The Laughter Company shows were eventually moved to Wednesday nights and the owner of the Eastside Comedy Club increasingly found weekend work for O'Donnell in the tri-state area. On any given weekend, O'Donnell could be found performing in Buffalo, New York; Trenton, New Jersey; or Wilmington, Delaware. Typically she received $110 per night.

Once she began traveling on the comedy circuit, there was no holding O'Donnell back. If anyone mentioned the name of a possible contact anywhere in the country, O'Donnell would immediately grab a phone and attempt to sell her talents to the club's owner.

The Perils of a Young Woman on the Road

Even for a hard worker like Rosie O'Donnell, the life of a stand-up comedian was not easy. She received little encouragement from her family and friends. Time and time again people would tell her to quit. O'Donnell talked about this lack of support in the January/February issue of *Ms.* magazine. "People would say, 'You're too tough to be an entertainer. You're too heavy to be famous.' I always thought to myself, 'You don't know who I am. *I* know.'"[29]

By the mid-1980s, O'Donnell was touring the United States as a stand-up comedian at colleges and clubs. Her act was as popular as any of the others, but she was getting paid much less than her male counterparts. O'Donnell discovered this one night after she had become a headliner. She was friendly with the woman who kept the books for a club where she was working. According to the book *Rosie:*

> The woman said, "There must be a mistake here. It says you're only getting seven hundred dollars to headline. It must be seventeen hundred, right?" I was getting less than half of what a man would get.[30]

Along with the pay inequities, the life of a stand-up comedian was far from glamorous. To save money, club owners would rent cheap rooms, called "comedy condos," that were kept for the sole use of traveling comics. Most of the comics were men who didn't feel obligated to pick up after themselves, and the clubs did not spend much money on housekeeping. O'Donnell describes the comic's life in vivid detail in Gloria Goodman's *The Life and Humor of Rosie O'Donnell:*

> You'd arrive in town and they'd have a kid come pick you up in a used Vega . . . with a door that didn't close. You'd have to get in on the driver's side and climb over his lunch from Hardee's. All of us would be scrunched in the backseat, and he'd take us to this filthy condo where we would all live for days, with sheets that have to be shaved because they all had little bumps on them, with rotten leftover takeout food in the fridge and shower curtains with mold. Very disgusting.[31]

But O'Donnell was in her early twenties and loved getting paid to make people laugh. There was plenty of excitement in the life of a comedian, but also fear. According to *Rosie O'Donnell: Her True Story:*

The other comics were much older. They'd pick up women at the bars [and] bring them home. . . . I was like twenty and totally freaked out from hearing these noises through the wall. I put the dresser up against the door. Everybody was doing drugs and drinking, and I was just this little girl on the road, scared in her room. With cocaine the drug of choice back then, it was not uncommon for a comic to stop by the club office after a gig to collect their pay and be asked if they wanted to be paid in "green [money] or white [cocaine]."[32]

O'Donnell says that there were only about six women working the circuit when she began (she says there might be six hundred today). Not only were 99 percent of the comics men, but so too were the managers, producers, agents, and network people. Life for a woman on the road was particularly tough going. A typical comic's life consisted of driving from town to town at night, parking in dark, isolated parking lots, walking alone into smoky nightclubs, and taking control of a room full of drunk strangers to tell them jokes. This was difficult enough for a man, but for a woman traveling to crime-ridden cities, it could be particularly intimidating. O'Donnell rarely shrank from a tough challenge, however, because she wanted show-business success badly enough to face down her fears.

Inclusive Comedy

O'Donnell traveled the comedy circuit, cracking people up by mimicking her father's Irish brogue and joking about her Irish Catholic upbringing. Other routines included her classic exercise routine in which she joked about her fluctuating weight. Another mainstay of her act consisted of jokes about pop-culture trivia such as television shows and show-business celebrities.

While on the road, O'Donnell would keep a small notebook with her to record her observations about people she met. She took the notebook to shopping malls, McDonald's restaurants, and movie theaters. She also stayed away from vulgar comedy at a time when many comedians such as Andrew Dice Clay were hitting it big by making fun of women, gays, and minorities. As O'Donnell said: "I make fun of what I know best: Growing up in a big family, learning not to hate your stepmother, dieting, listening to a four-year-old try to tell a joke—that kind of stuff."[33]

O'Donnell proved exceptional in more ways than just being funny. Her good manners and professional behavior made a favorable impression on club personnel and her fans. It was common for O'Donnell to sit for two hours after a show to sign autographs for every customer who was leaving. She would also talk with each person for a minute, and kiss and hug everyone on the way out. Some nights O'Donnell gave this treatment to five hundred people. Because of this O'Donnell never "bombed" with her routine. She was simply too well liked for the audience to boo her if her jokes did not get the laughs she intended.

The Comedy Boom

The young Rosie O'Donnell originally wanted to become an actress, *not* a stand-up comedian. Although she could not have guessed it when she was practicing comedy in high school, the 1980s would prove to be a boom time for stand-up comedy. By the mid-1980s almost every big city and many smaller towns had a comedy club with a name such as Nyuk-Nyuks or the Laughter Zone. At the peak of the craze there were more than fifteen hundred comedy clubs in the United States. With each club booking several acts a night, there was a shortage of comics to fill the huge demand.

With the growth in the comedy business, it was more common for a stand-up comedian to earn a living playing the "laugh circuit." At this time cable television was just beginning to grow in popularity. (Cable TV did not exist at all until the late 1970s.) Engagements on the comedy circuit led to work on cable TV, once programming directors found that stand-up comedy was an inexpensive way to fill unused airtime and get viewers to tune in. And because cable shows were uncensored, comics did not have to rewrite their material to get it on the air. Another factor in comedy's growing popularity was the late-night debut in 1982 of *Late Night with David Letterman*. Letterman, a sympathetic veteran of the stand-up comedy circuit, booked many cutting-edge comedians for his show.

All these factors combined in the 1980s to provide comics with the potential to become household names and secure work in feature films and television shows.

Even O'Donnell's sweet personality could fail her occasion-
ally, and one time when she displayed a more cynical attitude,
it threatened her career. When O'Donnell was playing in a Long
Island comedy club one night in 1984, a young woman approached her and asked if she wanted to be on *Star Search*.
O'Donnell, a self-confessed "TV junkie," must have been aware
of the new popular talent show hosted by Ed McMahon. But
O'Donnell thought the woman was kidding and answered in dis-

*Mimicking her father's Irish accent and joking about her fluctuating
weight were just a few ways Rosie made the audience laugh.*

Making People Laugh for Free

Back in the 1960s, there was only one showcase comedy club in the entire country—Manhattan's Improv. The Improv readily booked raw and untested talent whereas other nightclubs booked only established comics, if any at all, as opening acts for singers. By 1975, the Improv had presented more than ten thousand new acts, including such stand-up greats as Bill Cosby, David Brenner, and Freddie Prinze. Unfortunately for the performers, it was against house rules to pay the comics—all they received was free drinks from the bar.

The Comedy Store was opened in Los Angeles in 1972 by Mitzi and Sammy Shore (parents of Pauly Shore). Some of the comics who worked there became legends: David Letterman, Richard Pryor, and Robin Williams. Like its New York cousin, the Comedy Store also re-fused to pay comics. But L.A.'s Comedy Store became the place for talent bookers to check out new comics. Some of them got a break and were invited to appear on *The Tonight Show* with Johnny Carson.

In 1979, comics realized that the Comedy Store was bringing in $2.5 million a year in ticket sales. They went on strike and demanded to be paid. The comedy strike ended when comics were promised $25 a set. The idea of paying comics spread to the Improv and other, smaller clubs. When promoters realized that comedy clubs could pay enter-tainers and still be profitable, they began taking over fading saloons and dance halls from coast to coast. The number of clubs nationwide jumped from ten in 1980 to three hundred in 1986. As luck would have it, this was about the time Rosie O'Donnell chose to make her living making people laugh.

belief, "Oh yeah, sure."[34] As it turned out, the woman inviting O'Donnell to appear on national television was McMahon's daughter, Claudia. When it became clear who Claudia McMahon was, O'Donnell apologized. Then she signed up for the next step in her career—broadcast television.

Chapter 3

Television Breakthrough

JUST AS SUCCESS is sometimes portrayed in the movies, Rosie O'Donnell got her big break in a talent contest, on Ed McMahon's show *Star Search*. (McMahon was best known at the time for being Johnny Carson's sidekick on *The Tonight Show*, which opened every night with McMahon's famous announcement "And heeeeeeeere's Johnny!") O'Donnell landed a spot on *Star Search* after she was chosen as one of 160 acts—out of 20,000 would-be entertainers who attended open auditions in forty cities.

Being chosen as an act on Ed McMahon's show was a huge opportunity for an entertainer. But a lot of comics were reluctant to appear on *Star Search*. Although it was an amateur show the competition was tough. Moreover, comics had only ninety seconds to win over the audience—and the judges.

First Woman to Win Comedy Category

O'Donnell did win, and she dethroned the reigning champion (an unknown who was never heard from again). In the show's short history, O'Donnell was the first woman to win the comedy category. With her thick Long Island accent and big, curly 1980s hairdo, O'Donnell was a hit and went on to defend her championship status four times. Although she didn't go on to win the $100,000 prize, she did win $20,000. Since she had been living in a cheap Hollywood hotel and living on hot dogs during the entire time she appeared on the show, the prize represented a huge amount of money for her.

Reality Check

O'Donnell took her *Star Search* prize money and moved from Long Island to Los Angeles, where she continued to work comedy clubs. She also spent some of the money to get her teeth crowned (for those hoped-for movie close-ups). But reality set in quickly when the comedian returned to Los Angeles; offers for parts in films did not come flooding in. "I thought that after I did *Star Search*," O'Donnell told an interviewer, "[Director Steven] Spielberg would be at home going, 'She's the next girl in E.T. 2.'"[35]

The lack of immediate success in the movie business may have been disappointing, but Hollywood was a town where even big stars like Robin Williams continued to work at the Improv to hone his act. Finishing as a semifinalist on *Star Search* wasn't going to impress Hollywood talent bookers. Ironically, years later when Ed McMahon was asked who the most famous person was to ever appear on his show he said: "I would have to guess Rosie O'Donnell, because of the variety of successes in cable, movies, etc."[36]

O'Donnell had not reckoned that while *Star Search* was very popular in some parts of America, it was looked down upon by Hollywood producers as being unsophisticated. Frustrated by the lack of offers, O'Donnell worked the Los Angeles comedy clubs, but she still could not get booked at showcases like the Improv. There was just too much competition from dozens of up-and-coming comedians—the downside of the comedy boom. Besides, it was still a business mostly run by men—few women were allowed to perform in major venues.

Eventually O'Donnell did get booked for the first time as a headliner, not in Los Angeles, but the Comedy Castle in Detroit, Michigan. Although her *Star Search* credentials got her a headline spot, the first time she performed she could not connect with the Detroit audience. And she was following a hot young Detroit native who was slaying the audience with his tool-guy-grunt shtick—future *Home Improvement* star Tim Allen. When she followed Allen the audience heckled her by chanting, "Tim, Tim, Tim." For succeeding shows, O'Donnell asked Allen to switch places with her, and that change proved to be a lifesaver

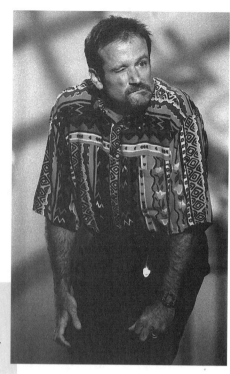

Rosie performed on the Los Angeles comedy club circuit, where even big stars like Robin Williams worked to polish their acts.

for O'Donnell. Had she failed at the Comedy Castle, word would have gotten around to other clubs, and she might never have headlined again.

Another Big Break

Over the next several years, O'Donnell used her *Star Search* credentials to book her act into dozens of comedy clubs around the country. She toured up and down the West Coast, returned to Michigan a few times, and got some star bookings at several casinos in Atlantic City, New Jersey. O'Donnell also opened for some big-name acts including soul group the Temptations, magician David Copperfield, and country singer Dolly Parton.

Slowly but surely, O'Donnell was making her mark in show business. Her next big break came when she was working a date at Igby's Comedy Club in Los Angeles. O'Donnell was appearing with Montana-born comic Dana Carvey. In the audience to see

Carvey that night was NBC president Brandon Tartikoff and *Saturday Night Live* producer Lorne Michaels. O'Donnell's manager asked the network executives if they would stay to see Rosie.

Tartikoff and Michaels stayed for O'Donnell's act, and the comedian worked a bit into her routine pleading with the startled Tartikoff to give her a break. Both O'Donnell and Carvey were lucky that night. Carvey was given a spot on *Saturday Night Live,* and O'Donnell was offered a role on an NBC comedy series.

Gimme a Break

While Tartikoff was watching O'Donnell's act, he had a brainstorm: Perhaps this brash young woman would provide a jolt of energy to the long-running sitcom *Gimme a Break,* which was losing some of its popularity with viewers. Tartikoff introduced himself and told O'Donnell he wanted to cast her on the TV show. Her reaction, as related in *Rosie,* by James Robert Parish was "Yeah, right! Come on. He's not going to do that. That's the

O'Donnell learned that following Tim Allen at a Detroit comedy club was a dangerous thing to do.

kind of story you read about in a Hollywood newspaper."[37] Tartikoff, however, was very serious about his offer. His show needed help, and he thought Rosie O'Donnell could provide it.

Gimme a Break had first gone on the air in 1981. It was a show about the difficulties experienced by a widowed, middle-aged white police chief with three growing daughters. The chief hired a black woman to be his housekeeper. Before long, the housekeeper, played by Nell Carter, and the chief, played by Dolph Sweet, were engaged in a never-ending battle of wits. Each show featured one character or the other trying to assert authority over the household. The show had never made it into the top twenty-five shows in television's ratings but had remained popular enough to be renewed each year.

Disaster struck *Gimme a Break* when Dolph Sweet died of cancer in 1985. Viewers wondered if the show could go on without one of its lead characters. Several new characters had been introduced, but the show seemed lost without Sweet. Instead of calling it quits, Tartikoff decided to introduce the twenty-four-year-old O'Donnell to the mix. She joined the cast for the 1986–87 viewing season, playing the part of Maggie O'Brien, Nell's upstairs neighbor. O'Donnell described the role as "Rhoda Morgenstern with an Irish accent."[38]

Gimme a Break was always teetering on the brink of cancellation, in part because the network kept moving it around in the schedule. During its run it played at ten different time slots on four different nights. The last year with O'Donnell it played on two different nights at two different times. Fans of the show found it difficult to find the program.

In spite of its difficulties, the show provided O'Donnell with an apprenticeship in TV acting. She learned the technical basics such as moving around the set, making snappy entrances and exits, playing the camera in different ways, and meshing with other actors. In a sense *Gimme a Break* allowed O'Donnell to complete the drama course she had never finished in college— this time with several million people watching.

Unfortunately, O'Donnell found herself caught in the middle of ego clashes and political feuds that had been flaring up

Rosie Gives Up Drinking

Working on the set of the failing sitcom *Gimme a Break* caused Rosie O'Donnell a lot of anxiety. Another source of discomfort was that she had recently quit drinking alcohol. O'Donnell had started drinking a lot when she was a young comic. All the male comics she was working with were much older than she, so instead of going back to the motel where she would be fearful and kept awake by their partying, O'Donnell stayed behind in the comedy clubs to drink with the waitresses, trying to make herself sleepy. James Robert Parish picks up the story in *Rosie:*

> Adding to Rosie's discomforts on the sitcom set [of *Gimme a Break*] was the stress due to her efforts to stop drinking. (One acquaintance at the time would recall that Rosie had a fondness for drinking quickly three or four beers then having a chaser shot of Jameson's Irish Whiskey.) Years later, Rosie would confide, "When I moved to L.A. and got on a sitcom, a friend of mine said, 'You drink too much, and you've had a lot of alcoholism in your family.' I was so mad. I said, 'Are you implying that I'm an alcoholic?'" O'Donnell adds, "She was a therapist, this friend, and she said, 'I just think you have a problem.' So I stopped drinking totally for 5 years, just to show her I could. And I think it's good that I did, because if I had continued along the way that I was, I seriously feel that it would have become a problem for me."

between other cast members for years. But she was well liked and provided much-needed comic relief.

Gimme a Break was canceled at the end of O'Donnell's one and only season on the show. The dream of appearing on a sitcom had turned into a bitter reality for the actress. O'Donnell said of this time:

It was the most crushing blow of my career. My goal was to be on a sitcom; then I got on this show in its last year and people weren't ready to be there. I thought I've climbed this mountain and there's nothing there.[39]

Having been on the show, however, gave O'Donnell new credibility with the casting agents who book talent for TV shows and movies. It had also helped attract new people to O'Donnell's stand-up performances.

O'Donnell was not very happy in the months after *Gimme a Break* was canceled. Soon it was necessary to go back on the road as a stand-up comedian, something she thought she had moved beyond. But returning to her roots in the comedy clubs restored her spirits. Where before O'Donnell had to struggle to get bookings, now that she was fresh from a sitcom, clubs were happy to have her. Furthermore, she was getting more money per appearance. After being rejected for two years by the L.A. Improv, she was now welcomed with open arms. In fact the owner, Bud Friedman, steered her toward her next television job.

From Sitcom Actress to Veejay

Friedman had heard that MTV was looking for a female veejay (music video program announcer) to give hip, funny commentary between music videos. Other female comics had turned down the offer, feeling that viewers were only tuning in to watch their favorite rock bands, not see a comedian. O'Donnell felt different about the offer:

> I needed a change, a new challenge. I saw it as an opportunity to let a lot of people know me and distinguish me from the many female comics who were working the circuit.[40]

The producers of MTV didn't think O'Donnell fit the image of the "thin, young, heavy-rocker." But they liked O'Donnell's style and suggested her for a similar slot on VH1 (Video Hits One). VH1 had been on the air since 1985 and was trying to appeal to an older audience than its sister station MTV. O'Donnell may not have been hip enough for MTV, but she seemed to provide exactly what VH1 needed.

Most of O'Donnell's fellow comedians did not think becoming a veejay was a good career move, calling it a leap into obscurity. In fact many comics made fun of VH1 every night in their acts. But, as O'Donnell later told *Entertainment Weekly:* "Everyone told me not to do it, and I did it anyway. There's no map to get to success in this industry—you have to take a knife and hack your way through the jungle."[41]

On the plus side, VH1 reached 28 million homes, which meant excellent exposure for her. And O'Donnell was tired of the

Rosie's Rules for Finishing First

Rosie O'Donnell has rules that have helped her become successful. They were printed in the article "Miss Congeniality," by Melina Gerosa, in the February 1997 issue of *Ladies' Home Journal*.

ROSIE'S RULES: How This Nice Girl Finished First

Be Friendly to Everyone

She landed her first acting job, a role on the sitcom *Gimme a Break*, with the help of a cocktail waitress she befriended at one of her regular comedy gigs. Because O'Donnell had always been nice to her, the waitress refused to give a table of NBC executives their check until they'd seen O'Donnell's act.

Mind Your Manners

After her veejay audition tape was rejected by MTV, O'Donnell still wrote the producer a nice note. He was so impressed by the gesture that he hooked her up at VH1, where she landed a coveted veejay job. "A thank-you note got me that job," she says.

Play Nice

The comedian will only tell jokes about somebody that she would feel comfortable saying to them—the exceptions being O. J. Simpson and Woody Allen. "If I'm morally offended by somebody . . . you're open game," she says. "But I've never been interested in mean-spirited comedy." An audience-pleasing move, considering her show is the highest-rated debut of daytime talk shows in the last decade.

Forgive and Forget

When Donny Osmond made a fat joke on her show, he was booed off the stage. Still, the host invited him back to apologize. "I made him put on a puppy-dog suit and sing 'Puppy Love,'" she says. "It was the highest-rated show ever."

road. As a veejay, she would be living in New York, where she would be able to see more of her family. She missed her brothers and her sister, Maureen, who now had a young daughter.

In April 1988, at the age of twenty-six, Rosie O'Donnell began introducing Top 40 rock videos on VH1. It was a full-time job that required O'Donnell to write twenty-four three-minute

The Comedy Glut

In the 1980s, the world of stand-up comedy changed from unknown comics joking for free to an explosion of comedy clubs and TV specials. Rosie O'Donnell rode this comedy wave to celebrity success. But what started out as quirky comedy alternatives soon turned into a glut. George Mair and Anna Green discussed this issue in *Rosie O'Donnell: Her True Story:*

> One reviewer at the time put it this way: "Comedy is no longer seen as relief from everyday life, a respite from the stress of workaday activity. Cable TV is turning humor into just another unavoidable part of existence, an unrelenting fact of life from which drama now beckons as a welcome alternative." Given this glut of programming, it's not surprising that the quality began to decline sharply.
>
> Chick Perrin of the Comedy Connection shares his theory on the change. "It's just typical of Hollywood—they overkill everything. The very thing that made comedy a hit in the eighties was the thing that killed it in the nineties. We see people that I don't even know on HBO specials, and they suck. So it's just a big cycle. They always kill the golden goose." The very economy of putting on comedy shows meant there weren't enough good comics to go around. As a result mediocre talent got pushed to the head of the line. In turn many paying customers stopped going to the clubs, especially when they could stay home and watch all the comedy they wanted on television.

comedy segments seven days a week. The bits played between the music videos. It was an odd experience for O'Donnell because there was no audience for her to interact with—she couldn't tell if she was going over or not. In one of the funnier pieces, she has a dialogue with the cameraman, who responds yes or no by tilting or shaking the camera.

O'Donnell liked the veejay gig. She said at the time, "I get to talk about my life, my weight, Whitney Houston's ego problems, whatever pops into my head. It sure beats working for a living."[42] And the nonstop schedule of three-minute bits helped O'Donnell expand her comedy repertoire. She later recalled:

That was hard work, but it was very valuable. It taught me
to draw on all my resources, to pay attention to everything,
so I can use it. It was like high-impact comedy aerobics.[43]

Rosie the Producer

Despite O'Donnell's success, VH1 decided to phase out all of
their veejays. Since O'Donnell's contract had not expired, the
station offered to pay her the money she would have earned
over the remaining time of the agreement. Instead of leaving,
however, O'Donnell was determined to make this experience
the big break that would lead her to something better.
O'Donnell made the station a brilliant counteroffer—she would
produce a stand-up show and they could continue to pay her the
same money as they had for the veejay gig. If the show was a
success, they would extend her contract and raise her salary.

Executives at VH1 figured they had nothing to lose, so on
November 19, 1989, *Stand-up Spotlight* went on the air with
O'Donnell acting as producer. The show quickly went on to be-
come VH1's highest-rated program for several years.

The *Stand-up Spotlight*'s format was simple. O'Donnell
opened each show with her own comedy monologue. She was
followed by two established comedians and one up-and-coming
comic. This gave O'Donnell and the other comics enormous exposure because the show was aired sixteen times a week to an
audience that eventually grew to 36 million households.

As a producer O'Donnell was able to control the content,
pace, timing—the whole feel of the show. She reviewed tapes
from hundreds of aspiring comics across the country, helped book
the talent, and gave some of her old friends in the comedy clubs
their first break on TV. Her other duties included budgeting
money for the show, scheduling the logistics of taping the show,
working with the technicians, and arranging for backup comics in
case a booked comic didn't show up for a taping session.

O'Donnell also introduced a friendliness to the production
process that was unheard of in the tough world of stand-up comedy.
She made sure each comic received a fleece robe with "VH1" em-
broidered on it and an embossed travel bag. Comics who appeared

O'Donnell became adept at many aspects of show business, from stand-up comedy to TV producing.

on the show felt they were treated like royalty. Even if they didn't get their next big break they felt good about their experience.

O'Donnell thrived in her new role. She said at the time:

> I've spent years developing my own act, and now producing *Stand-up Spotlight* lets me cultivate new talent and help other people develop their careers. I love coming up with concepts, then working to make them happen. It's very exciting and a lot more fun than I ever imagined behind-the-scenes work could be.[44]

O'Donnell's work on *Stand-up Spotlight* paid her big dividends professionally. She received her first award nominations—an American Comedy Award and a Cable Ace Award. In addition, VH1's parent company, Viacom—which owned the Showtime premium cable network—signed O'Donnell to appear on "Showtime's Comedy All-Stars," and several other high-paying specials.

As the 1980s drew to a close, O'Donnell no longer had to rely for her livelihood on the uncertainties of the stand-up comedy world. Her lucrative backstage work put her far ahead of the crowd of new comedians anxious to cash in on the comedy glut. But after an ill-fated job as a costar on the TV sitcom *Stand by Your Man* (canceled after four short months), O'Donnell decided that she was ready to leave television for a shot at her childhood dream—starring in big-screen Hollywood movies.

Rosie the Movie Star

Althought the sitcom *Stand by Your Man* was a failure for O'Donnell in 1992, the comedian was still in demand on an ever-growing list of TV specials, charity benefits, and talk show appearances. She helped out at Gloria Estefan's special on Showtime, "Hurricane Relief," and appeared on *Women Aloud,* an innovative cable series that featured women comics speaking out on the issues of the day. O'Donnell was also a guest star on what was one of TV's most popular shows at the time, *Beverly Hills 90210.* That appearance was a sure sign that O'Donnell was becoming a big name in Hollywood.

But 1992 would be remembered by O'Donnell as the year she premiered in her first movie and made a name for herself on the big screen. The ups and downs of Hollywood stardom, however, would also take a toll on the actress.

A League of Their Own

O'Donnell was an athlete in high school, and she couldn't decide whether she wanted to be a great performer or a great athlete. So it was perfect casting when O'Donnell was chosen to portray a baseball player in *A League of Their Own,* a film about the All-American Girls Professional Baseball League. In another twist, O'Donnell had always wanted to play a role like that of Laverne De Fazio in the sitcom *Laverne and Shirley,* which ran on TV from 1976 to 1983. So it was perfect for O'Donnell that *A League of Their Own* was to be directed by Penny Marshall, the actress who had played Laverne.

O'Donnell had started playing baseball when she was five years old. There were twenty-three boys on her block and only

46

The All-American Girls Baseball League

Until the movie *A League of Their Own* was released, many people thought that professional baseball had always been a man's sport. But back in the 1940s, millions of men were drafted to fight in World War II, creating a shortage of male athletes. Of the 5,700 men who played in the major and minor leagues in 1941, more than 4,000 of them eventually served in the military. The number of minor-league teams shrank from forty-one at the start of the war to nine during the war. The player shortage threatened to shut down professional baseball.

The prospect of no professional baseball was unacceptable to Phillip K. Wrigley, who owned the chewing gum empire as well as the Chicago Cubs. Wrigley and a few other businessmen spearheaded a drive to create the All-American Girls Professional Baseball League, which numbered ten teams. The experiment was popular throughout World War II and even afterward. But when the men came home from war, the women's league began to falter in popularity, finally quitting operations in 1954.

By the late 1950s, the women's league was all but forgotten. But when the players were inducted into the Baseball Hall of Fame in Cooperstown, New York, in 1958, several articles were written about this unique squad of players. In 1988, Kelly Candaele, the daughter of one of the players, made a documentary about the women athletes called *A League of Their Own*. When the players later had a reunion, two Hollywood film producers attended and bought the screen rights to the documentary film. Penny Marshall joined with the producers, and went on to direct the 1992 full-length feature film version.

A real girls' baseball league team from Chicago.

Among members of the cast of A League of Their Own, *Rosie was one of the few who had really played baseball.*

six girls, so O'Donnell had to be good in order for her to compete with the boys. When casting for *A League of Their Own* began, every woman who auditioned for the film also had to pass tryouts to prove she had the athletic ability to portray a baseball player. To evaluate the women, the producers hired Rod Dedeaux, a veteran University of Southern California (USC) and Olympic baseball coach. The recruiting took place in Los Angeles, New York, Chicago, Toronto, and Atlanta.

Almost every famous, able-bodied actress in Hollywood tried out for the movie. The women were videotaped hitting, running, catching, and throwing. O'Donnell was quite amused by what she saw. She was quoted in *Rosie:*

> It was really funny to see all these actresses who had never played baseball who had lied to their agents and said "Oh, yeah, I can play." Like, you know, these really thin Barbie doll-like women. And I'm like "Honey, hold the thin end of the bat, OK? Good luck. . . . Be careful out there. . . . When I read the script, I thought, "If I

don't get this part, I'll quit show business." If there's one thing I can do better than Meryl Streep and Glen Close, it's play baseball.[45]

O'Donnell was cast to play third base in the film. In a 1997 interview with *Ladies' Home Journal,* O'Donnell quipped: "I was the only one who could throw the ball from third to first, so I got the job."[46]

O'Donnell played Doris Murphy, but the role was written "for a hot, sexy girl." Once O'Donnell joined the cast, the part was rewritten. "We changed the script to make a part for her," said director Penny Marshall. "She had a wonderful quality. And besides, she could play baseball."[47]

Rosie and Madonna

Madonna was also eager to land a part in the film. So eager, in fact, that she hired baseball great Jose Canseco to coach her. It wasn't necessary. Marshall wanted Madonna in the movie and was worried about auditioning for *her.* Marshall put the pressure on O'Donnell to help recruit Madonna for the movie. "Be funny," Marshall urged Rosie. "If she likes you and she likes me, she'll do the movie."[48]

Madonna did take the part, and O'Donnell was cast as her best friend. Before the filming began, O'Donnell was terrified of meeting a huge celebrity like Madonna. In fact she was nauseous for two hours before the meeting. But after seeing the singer's movie *Truth or Dare,* especially the scene in which Madonna mourns for her dead mother, O'Donnell knew she and Madonna were kindred spirits. At their first meeting, O'Donnell recalls, "I looked her right in the eye and said, 'My mom died when I was ten, too. Your movie reminds me a lot of my life.' And that was it. We became friends right then."[49]

Madonna commented on her friendship with O'Donnell in the July 1996 issue of *Life* magazine: "Rosie and I speak the language of hurt people. She is very protective, loyal and maternal with me."[50] The antics of O'Donnell and Madonna added a bit of fun to the grueling work of making a movie about trained athletes.

Rosie and Madonna became good friends. Here they are watching a Phoenix Suns vs. LA Lakers game.

On the set, Madonna had this boom box. Somebody threw a ball at it, and she goes, "Hey! You break that, you're buying me a new one." I said, "Madonna, you have more money than most third world countries."[51]

O'Donnell worked hard on- and offscreen. The movie used five thousand extras to sit in the bleachers and cheer the team on. Some days the temperature on the set was more than 100 degrees. But, according to Marshall, when the extras became restless during the endless hours of setting up shots, O'Donnell would "take the microphone and do her stand-up and imitate Madonna singing 'Like a Virgin.'"[52] When O'Donnell was done, Madonna would rush out of the dugout and wrestle her to the ground.

A League of Their Own got good reviews and earned more than $107 million. O'Donnell won high praise for her role, as did the film, which helped put her on the trajectory to stardom.

Perhaps more important for her, O'Donnell came away from the film with two lifelong friends, Madonna and Penny Marshall.

Sleepless in Seattle

After her well-received role in *A League of Their Own*, Hollywood writers began to think of O'Donnell, as she has said, as the "sassy best friend with the heart of gold."[53] The roles she plays are so suited to her personality that it is easy for her to portray them. But when it comes to the actual craft of acting, the comedian says she never prepares.

O'Donnell's next movie, *Sleepless in Seattle*, was about the young son of a widower who tries to find a new wife for his father, played by Tom Hanks. The boy selects Meg Ryan, who does not even meet Hanks until the last scene in the movie.

Nora Ephron, who had written *Silkwood* and *When Harry Met Sally*, was selected to direct *Sleepless in Seattle*. Ephron remembers that before O'Donnell interviewed for the part she had never heard of the comedian. But O'Donnell wanted the part and would not leave Ephron's office until she put her in the movie (the actress was supposed to audition for ten minutes and stayed for more than an hour). Later that day, Ephron said to her children at dinner, "I saw this woman, I don't know if you've heard of her, she's on VH1. And they looked at me like, 'You're even older and more washed-up than we've dreamed,' and that was it."[54]

O'Donnell was cast as Becky, Ryan's boss and best friend. Instead of playing the loud, brash best friend, as in *A League of Their Own*, O'Donnell played her new role low key and deadpan. O'Donnell also had to moderate her thick New York accent for a character who was supposed to be a graduate from the Columbia School of Journalism. As on the set of *A League of Their Own*, O'Donnell kept the cast and crew in stitches. Ryan later said, "Whenever I saw that I'd be working with Rosie that day I knew I'd be having a blast and that my stomach would cramp because I'd be laughing so hard."[55]

The critics loved *Sleepless* and once again O'Donnell got rave reviews. Fans loved the film as well. The movie grossed $17 million during its first weekend, grossed more than $126 million in

Rosie and Meg Ryan in Sleepless in Seattle. *O'Donnell plays Ryan's boss and best friend.*

ticket sales, and $65 million in rentals. And O'Donnell received her first nomination for an acting award—an American Comedy Award for her second film.

Forgettable Films

Although O'Donnell was still involved with *Stand-up Spotlight,* the show was quickly becoming a less significant part of her career. Before long she was starring in another film, this time playing a district attorney in *Another Stakeout.* The movie was a detective comedy starring Emilio Estevez and Richard Dreyfuss. O'Donnell had to lie to get cast in the movie because the role required her to drive a souped-up stunt car. O'Donnell assured the producers she'd been driving stunt cars for years, though she didn't even know how to drive a stick shift at the time. *Another Stakeout* received mixed reviews, but O'Donnell did garner another nomination for an American Comedy Award.

O'Donnell went on to act in three films that did little to advance her Hollywood career. In the first two, *Fatal Instinct,* and *I'll Do Anything,* O'Donnell had insignificant parts. In the third film, *Car 54,*

Where Are You? O'Donnell's part was larger—and might have led her straight to the unemployment line. The movie was one of many trying to cash in on nostalgia for old TV sitcoms.

In the film, O'Donnell plays a foul-mouthed Brooklyn housewife who thinks her policeman husband is cheating on her. Unfortunately, this was O'Donnell's most substantial film role and one where she spent the most time in front of the camera. O'Donnell later said the movie "stunk" and was one of the worst experiences she had ever had in show business. O'Donnell had this advice for her fans: "You shouldn't rent it. If you do, I'm sorry and I owe you $1.50."[56]

Playing Betty Rubble

Luckily for O'Donnell, *Car 54* was overshadowed by her next, hugely popular movie, *The Flintstones*. This film was an attempt to take advantage of the popularity of another sixties sitcom, *The Flintstones* cartoon, which ran on ABC-TV from 1960 until 1966. The program was very popular and was brought back in 1972 and again in 1981. It led to other spin-offs such as *Pebbles and Bamm Bamm* (1971–76) and *The Flintstone Kids* (1986–88).

The Flintstones movie was a big-budget production, and every set was lavishly constructed to look like the original cartoon. But when O'Donnell was told that the producers wanted her for the part of Betty Rubble, she is quoted in *Rosie* as saying:

> I thought, are you kidding me? [Betty Rubble] is this tiny little petite thing, and I'm not exactly similar to the cartoon rendering in my own physicality. I didn't see it at first. Then when I went in and read [the script] and everyone laughed, I thought, OK. But I didn't lust after it my whole life, no. . . . I was [more] interested in playing Scooby Doo at one point.[57]

During the filming, O'Donnell got to work with another one of her idols, Elizabeth Taylor, who played Fred Flintstone's mother-in-law. As with other films she had been involved with, between takes O'Donnell would entertain the crew with a non-stop stream of jokes and show tunes.

Rosie as Betty Rubble in The Flintstones, *with Rick Moranis as Barney, John Goodman as Fred, and Elizabeth Perkins as Wilma.*

Reviewers panned the film, but *The Flintstones* grossed more than $200 million in ticket sales because the film was popular among youngsters. O'Donnell was named "Favorite Movie Actress" by Nickelodeon's Kids' Choice Awards for her role as Betty Rubble. Perhaps a greater honor for O'Donnell, who was an avid collector of McDonald's Happy Meal figurines, was for her character to be made into a Betty Rubble Happy Meal toy.

Rosie Bombs

After *The Flintstones,* Penny Marshall's brother, Garry, offered O'Donnell a role in a film called *Exit to Eden.* In this film, O'Donnell plays an undercover police officer who chases a smuggler to a remote island resort that is designed for romantic adventures. Once there, O'Donnell has to dress up like other vacationers, in a scanty leather fantasy outfit. Dan Aykroyd played the part of O'Donnell's partner.

In order to play the role, which was originally written for Sharon Stone, O'Donnell had to lose thirty pounds. When she found out that Stone had turned down the role, O'Donnell was stupefied that she had been chosen instead.

> I couldn't imagine the producers at this big meeting saying, "Shall we go with Sharon or Rosie? Sharon or Rosie?" she says with her distinctive bark of a laugh. I asked my agent, "How many people were offered the role between me and Sharon Stone? Ninety?"[58]

Weighing In on Weight

O'Donnell has continually struggled with her weight in a business where women starve themselves in order to work. She talked about the weight issue in depth with Kristen Golden in the January/February 1997 issue of *Ms.* magazine.

> To say that I don't struggle with weight issues is a lie—I do. I go between 150 and 200 pounds on a regular basis. But I don't think that I'm less of a person because I'm bigger than some people, nor do I think I'm better when I'm thinner. I just decided I didn't want to be part of that whole media message that makes little girls become anorexic.

O'Donnell became aware of the media's impact on children when she cohosted a special edition of *Nick News*, called *The Body Trap*, in 1996. Children talked with O'Donnell on how they felt about their bodies. O'Donnell asked the kids if they "would . . . rather be fat or have one arm?" Most kids said "one arm." O'Donnell's message on the show was that "people come in different sizes, shapes, and colors. I'm uncomfortable sometimes with my own body, but I'm never going to use it to demean myself, or to demean other women out there."

O'Donnell told *Ladies' Home Journal* in February 1997:

> Whenever anyone tells me to lose weight, I always laugh, like I *could*, but I'm just keeping it on because I *like* to! But when I'm at my thinnest, I never really feel thin. . . . So I'm disconnected from my career and my physical self.

Rosie at the New York premiere of The Flintstones.

But producer Marshall said there were no others because O'Donnell was adept at "mixing the comic with the erotic."[59]

Squeezing into the leather outfit was traumatic for O'Donnell, especially on the first day, when the camera crew made wisecracks about her look. At first she was afraid and embarrassed, but she finally got used to her role and, after a time, claimed to enjoy it. *Exit to Eden* was mercilessly panned by the critics, however. The humor fell flat and the sight of O'Donnell in black leather with whips and studs was more than many viewers could bear.

By the end of the experience, however, O'Donnell had acted in eight movies, six with substantial roles. In spite of her last film, she was in demand for even more films. She bought a home in the San Fernando Valley for $332,000 and began to make a comfortable life for herself in Hollywood.

Grease! on Broadway

In 1993, dancer, choreographer, and director Tommy Tune decided to bring his play *Grease!* back to Broadway. The play, which pays a tribute to the culture of the 1950s, had been very popular in the 1970s and was made into a movie in 1978. One of the characters in the play, Betty Rizzo, was a tough high school student who was the leader of a gang called the Pink Ladies.

When O'Donnell told the producers of *Grease!* she wanted the role of Rizzo, they were shocked. After starring in three hit movies (and a few duds) no one could believe O'Donnell wanted to play Broadway. But O'Donnell was signed on as Rizzo for a ten-month rehearsal period. And O'Donnell had her reasons for wanting to appear in the play: She is quoted in *Rosie:*

> The reason to do Broadway, for me, is because of my love for theater and how much it influenced my life and changed my career and goals, and just—it really enriched me as a child, and I hope to pass that on to other children who come to see this show. And it's really a family fun show and so the reason to do it is not the money.

As time wore on, the monotony of playing the same role on stage every night bored O'Donnell, and she left the production in 1994. Asked if she would ever do another play, she said, "Buy the [*Grease!*] CD, my days as a singer are over. Did they ever begin?"

O'Donnell tries her hand at a Broadway musical in Tommy Tune's Grease!

Moving Back to New York

The pace of life as a Hollywood star troubled O'Donnell. She explained the problems in *Rosie O'Donnell: Her True Story:*

> I find living in L.A., your whole life is centered around show business, and the more successful you become in it, the harder it is to get away from it. Living here, it doesn't stop. Every dinner. Every lunch. More and more meetings. It feeds on itself, and before you know it, there is no balance. All you have is work and very little life.[60]

In order to regain control of her life, O'Donnell sold her house and moved back to New York, where she had kept an apartment on the Upper West Side. It would be in New York that she would go on to take the world by storm with her very own television show.

Chapter 5

Rosie Hits the Big Time

AFTER MOVING FROM Los Angeles to New York and leaving behind the hectic world of Hollywood stardom, Rosie O'Donnell refused to remain idle for long. Even while filming movies and acting on Broadway, she found time to appear at a host of benefits, in comedy clubs, and on television.

In 1995, when O'Donnell accepted the Nickelodeon Kids' Choice Award, in a televised acceptance speech she said: "I

Rosie won the Nickelodeon Kids' Choice Award in 1995 for her role as Betty Rubble. She hosted the awards show in 1997 (shown).

want to tell you—all you kids here and all you kids at home—that you can live your dreams if you keep believing in yourself. So keep believing."[61] Although O'Donnell had fulfilled her dream of movie stardom, she was ready to get back to her roots on television. Once again she was in the right place at the right time.

Going Back to the Comedy Clubs

By 1995, O'Donnell was spending most of her free time trying out new comedy for her first one-woman TV special on HBO. To hone her material for the one-hour special, O'Donnell hit the road in the fall of 1995. Her first engagement was her old stomping grounds in Boston, where she performed for six nights. Next, it was on to Merv Griffin's Resorts Casino Hotel in Atlantic City, where O'Donnell performed her seventy-minute act three times for a fee of fifty thousand dollars.

O'Donnell's *HBO Comedy Hour* was taped at Boston's Faneuil Hall. It was the first time she had done a solid hour of stand-up on TV. The show aired on April 29, 1995. Critics loved the show, and it was replayed several times in subsequent months.

Following her successful TV special, O'Donnell was nominated for her first Emmy Award, for Outstanding Individual Performance on a Variety or Music Program. O'Donnell did not win the award, but ironically, it was captured by her childhood idol, Barbra Streisand, who won it for *her* TV special.

Adopting a Child

O'Donnell, who had come from a large family, was absolutely sure that she wanted to have children someday. She told the *Ladies' Home Journal:* "The same way I knew that I would be an entertainer [when I was young], I knew I would be a mother."[62] But, without a man in her life, O'Donnell was also sure she did not want to bear the baby herself. "I would be open to giving birth, but it wasn't in the near future when I started the [adoption] process," she says, adding, "I have no investment in having a miniature me running around."[63] O'Donnell's other reasons for not wanting her own child included a family history of alcoholism and other diseases such as the cancer that her mother died of.

Adoption had become something of a trend among Hollywood stars, with couples such as Tom Cruise and Nicole Kidman and Jamie Lee Curtis and husband Christopher Guest adopting children. In addition, many single women in the entertainment industry had adopted children, including Michelle Pfeiffer, Diane Keaton, Amanda Bearse (Marcy, on *Married with Children*), Sheena Easton, and Kate Jackson.

O'Donnell filled out adoption forms and waited. She admits that her celebrity status helped her obtain a baby very quickly. As she told an interviewer for *Life* magazine:

> You're given privileges whether you want them or not. I'm very conscious that most people wait much longer to adopt. But you wouldn't say, "No, thanks, I don't want that baby." I think you get the child you're supposed to have in your life.[64]

Parker Jaren O'Donnell was born on May 25, 1995. Rosie first saw him when her lawyer brought her a picture of the child, taken when he was one hour old. When Parker was just two days old, O'Donnell took him home. She described the experience in an interview with Liz Smith in *Good Housekeeping:*

> Because my mom died when I was a kid, my images of her were always idealized. I never really saw her as a woman. But when I first held my son in my arms, I had that overwhelming connection and a feeling of immense love that I never had before. I thought, My mother felt this for me. And for my siblings. So it was a really emotional time for me, those first few months with Parker, to connect with my mom and to think of her as a woman and not as my little girl's image of her.[65]

Without a mother to turn to for advice, O'Donnell relied on her friends to help her with Parker. She received a lot of help from actress Rita Wilson—Tom Hanks's wife—and Kate Capshaw, wife of Steven Spielberg. In spite of the new-mother jitters, O'Donnell was quickly convinced she had made the right decision. In an interview with *Redbook,* O'Donnell said:

Rosie with Parker and Parker's bottle.

I think all motherless children feel that having their own children will fill that hole in their lives. And Parker has done that for me. I feel like an adult for the first time.[66]

Back to the Movies

Motherhood changed how O'Donnell viewed her movie career. She still needed and wanted to work, but the roles she took on were smaller and demanded less of her time. In 1995, O'Donnell appeared in the film *Now and Then*, and in 1996 she appeared in *Beautiful Girls*. Both films received poor reviews and quickly dropped from sight.

After the huge success of *The Flintstones*, O'Donnell wanted to continue making movies for children. She told one interviewer:

When I did *The Flintstones* I saw the effect it had on little kids. It was really so pleasing to me to have a little six-year-old come up and go "Betty Rubble!" I loved it, and I thought it was a great kind of career to have. So I always tell my agent, if there are any kid movies that you see, let me know. I would love to be the person who made only kid movies.[67]

O'Donnell got her wish when she received a call to play Golly in *Harriet the Spy*. Based on the popular 1964 children's book by Louise Fitzhugh, *Harriet the Spy* is the story of an intelligent child and amateur writer who spies on her friends and family and writes about their activities in a private journal. Harriet's journal

Rosie and friends. O'Donnell has often used her fame and influence to help children.

Janie (Vanessa Lee Chester), Harriet (Michelle Trachtenberg), and Golly (O'Donnell) in Harriet the Spy.

is found by her classmates, who ostracize her. Golly is Harriet's wise nanny. She tells the young girl to continue to pursue her dreams even though others have turned against her. O'Donnell agreed to the role immediately because she had loved the book, which she felt, "encourages young girls to be independent and artistic and intellectual and strong."[68]

When *Harriet the Spy* was released in July 1996, critics were not greatly impressed. But the film had mass appeal and did fairly well at the box office, racking up $20.5 million in ticket sales. A good deal of the movie's success was attributed to O'Donnell's role in it.

Through her role in the movie, O'Donnell became a role model for young girls. Liz Smith asked her about it in *Good Housekeeping,* in 1997:

SMITH: You've become a heroine to millions of little girls since you appeared in the movies *Harriet the Spy* and *A League of Their Own.* How does that feel?

O'DONNELL: That's the best part of the whole thing. It's a heavy responsibility, though, the influence you have on them. It doesn't feel like a responsibility. It feels like an opportunity. When I was a kid I was influenced so much by movie stars and TV moms. I found a lot of solace and guidance from them. So the fact that I can now have a positive effect on little kids is wonderful. You can have a good effect, since you're not a blond cheerleader. You show them that anyone can accomplish what they want.

They really get me, these letters I get from little girls. They write things like, "Everyone used to tease me because I like to play baseball, but now they call me Rosie

Giving Autographs to Kids

O'Donnell does not like the fuss showered on her by adult celebrity seekers, but she understands the admiration of children. O'Donnell talked about it with Kristen Golden in *Ms.* magazine: "That's a pretty big thing, if you're a kid and you see Betty Rubble." In fact, O'Donnell will give autographs only to children. "When you're nine years old," she explains, "you take that autograph and you frame it or you tape it to your wall and you use it to dream of a better life than the one you know. It inspires you, it fosters creativity, it encourages you to believe in yourself. If you're 35 years old, what the hell are you gonna do with my name on a piece of paper?"

She later told Liz Smith in *Good Housekeeping:* "If I didn't draw the line, then every time I left my house I'd just be signing autographs." She told *Redbook* magazine:

> When Parker and I are walking through town and a little kid comes over and asks for an autograph, I say, "What's your name?" I say, "Hi, Mindy, you know what? I live in this town and you're gonna see me a lot. You're gonna see me at Little League, and at the school plays. So I'm not gonna be Rosie O'Donnell in this town. I'm just gonna be Rosie, Parker's mommy, okay?" And they always understand. I hear them as I walk past, telling each other, "She's not a star here, she's just Parker's mommy." And I feel so good.

after *A League of Their Own.*" The best letters are the ones where little girls say, "I used to think my mom was a nerd because she sings Barry Manilow and Elton John songs and talks about *The Partridge Family.* Now I think she's kind of cool."[69]

Landing a Talk Show Deal

In spite of her popularity, O'Donnell's life was focused on the care and feeding of an infant. The actress needed to make changes in her career that would allow her to spend most of her time with Parker. While filming *Harriet the Spy* in Toronto for twenty-six days, O'Donnell realized that she had to choose between full-time motherhood and making movies. And as luck would have it, the environment on TV was perfect for O'Donnell to make some positive changes in her career.

By the end of the 1993–94 television season, five of the top six shows on TV had stars who were former stand-up comics—and three of the five were women. Roseanne Arnold was a hit in *Roseanne,* Ellen DeGeneres was starring on *Ellen,* and Brett Butler starred in the popular *Grace Under Fire.* In addition Jerry Seinfeld was starring in the wildly popular *Seinfeld,* and O'Donnell's old stand-up buddy Tim Allen was in the equally popular *Home Improvement.*

Most of these comics had not been particularly well known until they landed their own shows, and TV executives were eager to sign O'Donnell, who had greater visibility than some other comics. But O'Donnell didn't want to move back to Los Angeles to appear in another (possibly short-lived) situation comedy. She knew exactly the kind of show she wanted—the kind she used to skip school to see when she was a kid—a daytime talk show. But she insisted that it had to be a show that she would feel comfortable with her child watching, not full of the abusive screaming and yelling on the "trash talk" shows like *The Jerry Springer Show* and others. As Rick Marin wrote in *Newsweek:*

> [O'Donnell] could not come across with the edgy, "college humor" of David Letterman or Conan O'Brian. And trash talk was out: "All [the trash-talk shows] give

these people [who appear] is a [plane] ticket to New York, and their shame is sold for that fee." [70]

O'Donnell had enough show-business savvy to know that she wanted to be the boss and own a large piece of her show —that was how Oprah Winfrey made her millions. To that end, O'Donnell started her own company, called KidRo Productions.

When the word was out that O'Donnell wanted to do a talk show, a bidding war ensued among Hollywood's biggest players, with each production company offering O'Donnell more money than the next. O'Donnell chose Warner Brothers and quickly signed a syndication contract reportedly worth $4.5 million a year—plus profits. O'Donnell also began with as much security as can be found on TV—with a commitment for thirty-nine weeks.

To practice for her new show, O'Donnell filled in for Greg Kinnear on NBC's early-hours show *Later*. She also filled in for Kathie Lee Gifford as the cohost on the *Live with Regis and Kathie Lee* morning talk show.

The Rosie O'Donnell Show

The Rosie O'Donnell Show was quickly picked up by TV stations across the country. The show was considered to be solid gold by station executives in many viewing markets. In some cities, several stations were bidding against each other to buy the show. Eventually *The Rosie O'Donnell Show* would be available for viewing in 97 percent of the United States.

O'Donnell was happy that she could produce the show in New York City. It meant she could live near her family, which included her brothers, who O'Donnell felt were important role models for Parker. It also meant that the show could be broadcast live on the East Coast.

On Monday, June 10, 1996, at 10:00 A.M., the thirty-four-year-old Rosie O'Donnell went on the air. All 180 seats in the studio at Rockefeller Center were full. O'Donnell had only a mild case of first-show jitters, and after her first guest, George Clooney, came on with an armful of roses, all was smooth sailing. From the very first show, it was obvious that O'Donnell was a different kind of talk show host. O'Donnell told Allison Adato in *Life* magazine:

> People shouldn't mistake it for a dysfunctional family show [like *Jerry Springer*]. It'll be a little monologue, a guest, maybe Susan Sarandon, a comedy piece, then, say, Garth Brooks to sing. I love his music. I'm much more middle America than anybody ever realized.[71]

O'Donnell's demeanor on her show quickly earned her the nickname "the Queen of Nice." As Kristen Golden wrote in *Ms.* magazine:

> She hugs her guest, she plugs their movies and CDs. . . . When O'Donnell's talent bookers come in the dressing room with a list of potential guests, the host says, "love 'em, love 'em, love 'em. There really hasn't been anyone I'm not thrilled with."[72]

Replacing Talk-Show Sleaze

A July 1996 article in *Newsweek* dubbed Rosie O'Donnell the "Queen of Nice." One of the reasons, according to *Newsweek* reporter Rick Marin, is that by 1996, people were tired of talk-show sleaze. Marin wrote:

> The . . . comedienne from New Yawk has gotten . . . cool stuff. . . . Great reviews. Big ratings. And credit for single-handedly saving daytime TV from itself. She's taken the trash out of talk by making nice, not nasty. And for that she should be given a Nobel Prize, or at least more Twinkies. . . .
>
> Not since Merv Griffin oozed his way through the '70s has there been this level of raw celebrity sycophancy [fawning, flattering behavior] on TV. Who'd have thought we'd be praising a talk-show host for being "the new Merv?" But it's such a relief from the freak-of-the-week sideshows on "Jenny Jones," or "Ricki Lake," "Sally Jessy Raphael" and their ilk. Warner Bros. put "Rosie" [on the air] to replace "Carnie," one of the many shameless "Ricki" clones that died this year. Bombarded with sleaze, viewers refused to watch "Carnie" . . . or any of their partners in slime.

The New Queen of Daytime TV

Audiences nationwide instantly fell in love with *The Rosie O'Donnell Show*. The program was attracting more than 3 million viewers a day during its first two weeks, making it the biggest debut since *Oprah*, ten years earlier. With top ratings in fourteen major TV markets, the comedian from Long Island suddenly gained big-time TV influence. Stations from coast to coast scrambled their schedules to give *The Rosie O'Donnell Show* their prime afternoon time slots—usually around 4:00 P.M. Television critics from *TV Guide* to the *New York Post* gushed with praise for O'Donnell.

Newsweek honored the new daytime talk-show queen with a spot on their cover under the headline "Queen of Nice." But O'Donnell was surprised at all the fuss. After she saw the magazine on the newsstands, she commented to *Ladies' Home Journal:* "You know how you can get your picture on a fake magazine cover? Every time I saw [the magazine] on a newsstand, I thought they'd put out a fake *Newsweek* that week."[73]

The show's popularity put O'Donnell on the endless celebrity lists that are loved by news shows and magazines. She was voted one of the hottest stars of the season by *Extra* in 1996. *Ladies' Home Journal* honored her as one of the "Most Fascinating Women of 1996." Her face appeared on the covers of dozens of magazines, including *Glamour, TV Guide*, a second *Newsweek, US*, and others. She was voted one of *Time* magazine's twenty-five most influential people in 1997. That same year she was voted one of the "50 Funniest People Alive" by *People* magazine. The young readers of *Seventeen* magazine even voted O'Donnell as their "ideal female president."

By the fall of 1996, O'Donnell's show was among the Top 20 of all syndicated shows. And her contract was renewed by Warner Brothers for her show to run through the 1999–2000 TV season. The next year, that contract was extended to 2001. By the 1997–98 television season, O'Donnell was a major celebrity and a household name. There were few changes planned for the show. But the prices the show charged advertisers for commercials were up 40 percent from the year before because

Rosie interviews one more personality on The Rosie O'Donnell Show.

O'Donnell's show attracted the young viewers that advertisers pay large sums to reach.

Rosie O'Donnell had finally made it to the top. She was on TV every day, just like her early heroes had been. She was paid millions upon millions of dollars every year. And she was one of the most beloved celebrities in America. With her life and future secure, O'Donnell turned her attentions to her true passions— her child, and a growing list of women's and children's charities.

Chapter 6

The Real Rosie O'Donnell

ROSIE O'DONNELL SPENT her entire life seeking the fame that is possible on the stage and screen. After she became rich and famous, however, O'Donnell started to tire of the spotlight. She wasn't prepared for the intense public examination of issues she thought of as personal, such as her weight and her tendency toward shyness.

As early as 1993, when success first came to her, O'Donnell said:

> Fame is like being hit by a tidal wave, and all you can do is try and keep your head above water. . . . Dealing with fame is hard for friends and relationships, and it's hard for love interests. But I have no regrets.[74]

But Parker has acted like an anchor for O'Donnell, because the reality of raising a child has given the comedian's life a basis in reality that can't be found in show business. As O'Donnell said to *Ladies' Home Journal:*

> [Parker's] taught me to value my time with him more than anything else. I leave work by three o'clock every day and turn the phones off until he goes to bed.[75]

Baby Chelsea

O'Donnell once said she wanted "a whole bathtub full"[76] of children. In October 1997, she told an interviewer with *Redbook* magazine:

Sports fans Rosie and Parker O'Donnell attend a Women's NBA game in New York.

I want to adopt another child, perhaps as early as next summer, and I may want to adopt more after that. I want Parker to be able to look over the bunk bed at his brothers and say, "Hey, doesn't it suck that Mom's on television?" I want him to have someone who understands. I mean, whenever we walk down the street, everyone knows his name. He has to think that's crazy as he gets older. So, hopefully, his siblings can roll their eyes with him.[77]

In fact, the occupant of the imaginary lower bunk mentioned in that interview was a very real baby girl that O'Donnell had adopted in secret. In September 1997, O'Donnell expanded her family by adopting a baby girl named Chelsea Belle, who has green eyes like her big brother's. Chelsea was secretly adopted to avoid publicity when she was only one week old.

O'Donnell had planned to surprise her family with the new baby at Thanksgiving that year but was forced to tell them two weeks early because Parker "blew her cover." "He was walking around telling people 'I got a new baby sister,'" O'Donnell laughs. "I kept saying 'He means baby-sitter.' But I couldn't go on lying to everyone."[78]

Fame and Its Rewards (and Drawbacks)

As *The Rosie O'Donnell Show* entered its second season, the monetary rewards of success were a source of enjoyment for O'Donnell. After all the cameras were turned off, the O'Donnell family often drove to Rosie's twenty-two-room, turn-of-the-century mansion in upstate New York. The house is huge—big enough to celebrate holidays with O'Donnell's sister, brothers, their kids, and friends. It is also secluded enough to keep out the paparazzi (celebrity photographers). "I have a fenced-in yard and swing set. My friends who have babies [including Madonna and Kate Capshaw] come over, and we don't have to be concerned with photographers."[79]

But O'Donnell remains true to her roots. She told *Ms.* magazine:

I'm the most uncelebrity celebrity. I go to The Gap and I'm in the back at the sale rack, and people say, "Why are you here? And *why* are you at the sale rack?" I don't know what people think—that you go shop at Barney's once you start making money? I don't feel any different.[80]

Rosie blows a bubble at a Hollywood show premiere.

Rosie's Brother Makes Bid for Congress

Rosie O'Donnell isn't the only public figure in her family. Her brother Daniel ran for the New York State senate in 1998. According to an article entitled "Out and Running," in *People Weekly*, May 4, 1998:

> Rosie O'Donnell's brother Daniel, 37, announced he will run as a Democrat—an openly gay one—for a seat in the New York State senate, representing Manhattan's Upper West Side and part of The Bronx.
>
> Rosie, 36, has long known about her brother's sexual orientation and, says Daniel, is "fine with it." He showed his political colors early. "The tip-off came when he was 8," Rosie says. "He founded a free legal clinic for the dolls he claimed I illegally evicted from my Barbie Dream House. . . ."
>
> While Rosie was winning *Star Search* competitions, Daniel was working his way through City University of New York law school. He did a seven-year stint in the Brooklyn public defender's office, and he continues to work for the rights of the underprivileged.
>
> Now, as he preps for the Sept. 15 primary, Daniel acknowledges his family connection is a double-edged sword. "People have said, 'You're only going to run because your sister's Rosie O'Donnell.' I say, 'It's not relevant that my sister happens to be

> famous.'" Rosie agrees. "He's one of the most selfless and dedicated people I know. He'll make a fantastic legislator."
>
> Although O'Donnell's campaign received quite a bit of publicity because of the candidate's famous sister, Mr. O'Donnell lost the primary on September 15.

O'Donnell's brother Daniel ran for the New York State senate.

Besides her house, O'Donnell's other big splurge was a twenty-seven-foot powerboat, which also provides her and the children with privacy. "I put a life jacket on Parker [and Chelsea]," O'Donnell says grinning, "and I drive around the island of Manhattan by the Statue of Liberty and Coney Island. He loves it, and it's a great way to get away from everyone. I had four hours of peace every day on the boat last summer."[81]

Of course fame's rewards come with some drawbacks. Intrusive tabloid newspaper reporters are a constant headache for O'Donnell. When asked if the coverage by gossipy tabloid newspapers has hurt her, O'Donnell answers: "I don't know that they've hurt me. But I definitely think they've shocked me. Listen, I mentioned on my show that I was on Fen-Phen (a diet drug) for a month after Parker was born. And the headlines read: 'Rosie's Fen-Phen Nightmare.'"[82]

Raising Kids

Although O'Donnell tries to keep her children out of the public eye, both of them cannot help but lead extraordinary lives. The unusual attention started right after Parker was adopted: Yankee baseball stars brought him autographed balls and bats; comedian Tim Allen gave him a kiddy tool belt; exercise guru Richard Simmons gave him a rhinestone-studded workout outfit; musician Kenny G presented him with a starter saxophone; Mr. Rogers dropped by Parker's neighborhood to play; and, of course, celebrity mothers brought their famous children by to spend time with the boy.

Like most mothers, O'Donnell wrestles with the issue of discipline. Having grown up in a house where there was no supervision from adults, the talk show host needed to set a few rules for her kids. When asked by *Good Housekeeping* if she gave her children time-outs, O'Donnell answered:

[I] do, but I don't know how effective it is. When Chelsea was younger, Parker would go over and hit her and then say, "I know, time-out." He'd walk over to his chair and sit in it and just wait. Then he'd ask, "Am I done?" It was in no way punishing to him. Now he's starting to understand bartering. The other day I said, "If you throw that toy, I'm going to take it away for good." He threw his toy and I took it away for good. Of course, you have to follow through. You see these moms at the mall saying, "If you yell one more time, we're leaving." Then the kid yells, and the mother stays. You're doomed if you do that.[83]

Like many single parents, O'Donnell has to worry about day care for her children. When O'Donnell's office started looking more like a toy store than a place of business, the talk show host used her clout at Warner Brothers to build a day-care center for all the show's employees. O'Donnell explained the need for the child-care center to Joanna Powell in the June 1998 issue of *Good Housekeeping:*

I'm a working single mother, and I took this job on a talk show so I could be with my kids. The first year, Parker was just a baby. But as he got older, it was hard to have him around during a meeting. He wanted to talk to me, wanted my attention. So I said we had to put in a school for him and the other kids. Warner Bros. wasn't very excited about it. There were insurance problems, and regulations that say a licensed day-care center can't be above the second floor, and we are on the eighth floor. There were all kinds of rules that I know many companies cite as reasons they can't provide a day-care center. But I said there had to be a way. People work very hard here. Not that they don't in factories. But they work hard and they never get to see their kids, and I didn't think it was right that I had my kid here every day and nobody else could.

We have two fulltime teachers, and the kids actually learn. It's very comforting for me. Next year Chelsea will come too. I'll bring her in the morning at 7:00, and Parker will go to another school from 9:00 to 12:00, then come back here until I'm done. In the afternoon, we'll all go home together.[84]

Rosie's Idea for Day-Care Centers

Rosie O'Donnell is lucky enough to have a day-care center at work so she can see her children during the day. Other parents are not so lucky, but O'Donnell has ideas to help them too. She explained her idea to Joanna Powell, in the June 1998 article, "Rosie's Devotion," in *Good Housekeeping* magazine:

> Studies have shown that 0 to 3 are the formative years for children, and I believe that's true. But for me it all comes down to money. I'd like to see mothers who are millionaires in this country each donate $1 million, which would go into an endowment account. You could take $50 million from it to fund day-care centers in inner cities to care for kids while their mothers work. It would be cooperative so that the parents had to come in and learn parenting skills. That's basically how to break the cycle of poverty, violence, and lack of nurturing with these kids. I'd love to get very right-wing and left-wing people who just care about children to come together for this.

In the article, she went on to advocate federal standards for day-care centers:

> The federal government needs to regulate who is able to open a childcare center, what has to be in it, and the safety standards. The caregivers have to be screened. . . .
>
> These days, parents have to work. Who's taking care of their kids? The most important investment our country can make in itself is to take care of its kids.

Raising Money for Charity

O'Donnell's concern for the lives of children extends beyond those of her own kids. In 1997, O'Donnell received a multimillion-dollar advance from Warner Books for a book entitled *Kids Are Punny: Jokes Sent by Kids to The Rosie O'Donnell Show*. O'Donnell used the money to set up a foundation to provide money for day care for children. She told Liz Smith in *Good Housekeeping* about the foundation:

> It's the For All Kids Foundation, which will fund different kinds of day care. Then, phase two will open new day-care centers and set a national standard. We're going to get a lot of moms in Hollywood to kick in money and get some corporate sponsors to match it.[85]

By January 1998, the For All Kids Foundation had handed
out an astonishing $1.5 million to 105 different children's chari-
ties. To raise more money, O'Donnell edited another book, *Kids
Are Punny 2;* the proceeds from the sale of which will allow the
foundation to continue giving away money for many years.

In 1998, O'Donnell explained to *Good Housekeeping* her reasons for giving so much to children:

> I'm haunted by the faces of children in need. The stories
> in the newspapers about abuse, the children who come
> on my show who have cancer . . . I see these kids' faces
> in my head every day. Kids are the only minority in this
> country who don't have a voice, legally. A kid in a house
> being abused or neglected often has no one to tell. Who
> takes care of those kids? Who gives them hope and in-
> stills the faith that life is a good thing? I don't think I can
> fix it all, but I cannot turn away from it. I feel a moral
> obligation to try to do something.[86]

*Rosie at the Kids' Choice
Awards in Los Angeles.*

O'Donnell also dedicates some of her time and money to AIDS charities, battered women's shelters, the Children's Defense Fund, and others. And like many other things in her life, O'Donnell credits her love of show business—and especially Barbra Streisand—for opening her eyes to others in need. She told Liz Smith:

> When I was a kid, Barbra Streisand was the most famous person to me, the person I most wanted to be. When my mother was sick, I thought: If Barbra Streisand's mother had cancer and everyone sent in a dollar, they'd find a cure. At 9 years old, I knew that with fame comes the power to change society—to cure diseases, to help people. When my mother died, I felt powerless—like there was nothing I could do to help. Now, I feel there are things I can do.[87]

Rosie O'Donnell plans to keep using her show as a forum to support the causes that are dear to her heart. One example of how this works is a deal O'Donnell made with the makers of Listerine mouthwash. In 1997, a Scope mouthwash–sponsored survey named O'Donnell the least kissable talk show host in America. In retaliation, O'Donnell endorsed Listerine. The makers of Listerine have donated $1,000 to charity every time Rosie was kissed on air by one of her guests. This agreement eventually placed more than $800,000 in the coffers of O'Donnell's children's foundation. In another product tie-in, Drake Bakeries (makers of Ring Dings, a fixture on the show) donated more than $100,000 for cystic fibrosis research.

O'Donnell On-Line

In addition to the time she spends with her kids, on her show, or with charity organizations, Rosie O'Donnell takes time for a hands-on approach to keeping in touch with her fans. O'Donnell's best friend since the age of two, Jackie Ellard, helps the comedian review and answer her mail. Ellard sorts the mail and answers special requests as best she can. She also sets aside special letters that she thinks O'Donnell should answer personally. There are

companies that specialize in answering mail for stars, but by en-
trusting this job to her friend, O'Donnell can be sure that she
will see the most important letters. But by 1998, O'Donnell was
receiving such a huge amount of mail that she found it hard to
respond to most letters.

O'Donnell is also an avid fan of the Internet, receiving more
than two thousand e-mail messages every day. (O'Donnell's e-
mail address is TheR0sie@aol.com (that's a zero in R0sie). She
is also reached by her fans through her home page at the Warner
Brothers website. In the past, she has even chatted with fans in
AOL chat rooms—sometimes using her real screen name
"TheR0SIE (with the zero), and sometimes anonymously, using
screen names such as "Lizard Lips" and "ROSIE OH O."

Sometimes O'Donnell would lie about her profession when
chatting on-line in order to have a normal conversation with
somebody. She justifies the lie by saying:

*Rosie and her dog
Buster.*

When you're famous, it's hard to have a conversation on equal terms. People have a preconceived idea of who and what you are. You're robbed of your ability to relate to people. Online, no one knows who you are.[88]

Periodically, O'Donnell holds live question-and-answer conferences on AOL. Hundreds of people type questions to a moderator, who then passes them along to O'Donnell, who in turn types her own answers. Sometimes, O'Donnell will just hang out in her own private chat room and exchange messages with whoever stops by.

O'Donnell often spends about an hour a day on-line typing letters to fans on her laptop computer. Rabid fans know that O'Donnell is most likely to pop into chat rooms late in the evening, after she has put her children to bed. Thanks to the AOL feature that helps locate another member on-line, fans can find out if O'Donnell is on-line. Once she has logged on, word spreads and before long, O'Donnell might be chatting with up to two hundred people.

Providing a Role Model

Because she sets an example through her personal life, the "Queen of Nice" has been called a perfect role model by magazines and TV news shows. But O'Donnell often tires of the label because she simply feels that she is doing what anyone in her situation should do. She told *Good Housekeeping:*

People say to me, "Oh you're a great mom, you're single, you're a role model." I'm not a role model. I'm a very, very rich woman who has the luxury of endless supplies of help. I'm the exception to every rule that there is about single parenting, and I shouldn't be held up as any sort of example. Very few people have the luxury I have in order to raise two children.[89]

Everything's Coming Up Rosie

By AUGUST 1998, *The Rosie O'Donnell Show* had been cruising along for two years as one of the top-rated shows on daytime TV. But the show faced big creative challenges as it headed into its third season. According to the entertainment industry magazine *Variety*, the show's national ratings were down more than 20 percent over 1997, and there was a growing chorus of critics who said that *The Rosie O'Donnell Show* had become predictable, and the antics of its host had grown stale.

In typical O'Donnell style, the talk show host and her producers addressed the issue head-on, filming a series of promotional spots in which O'Donnell earnestly listened to blunt advice from three sassy preteen girls, with one kid saying: "[Rosie], you gotta make some big changes." O'Donnell asks: "Am I still the host?" and the girl answers, "Well, for now." [90]

To bring viewers back to the show, O'Donnell has started to feature longer celebrity interviews and more segments on lifestyle and parenting-related topics. O'Donnell also began a new regular feature in which she chats with her biggest fans—children.

It's Been a Wonderful Ride

O'Donnell has said that "once you get fame you can never give it back. It affects everything. People come up and . . . it dehumanizes you. They think you're not human any more . . . but you can't really complain because you knew . . . it was going to be like this. And you get to be a millionaire, so what can I say?" [91]

John F. Kennedy Jr. shows the world his wedding ring on The Rosie O'Donnell Show.

In spite of the problems of celebrity, in her life off-camera, O'Donnell is a dedicated mother who basks in the joy and fulfillment that only family life can bring. She says that in the future she will probably adopt more children.

The best news for O'Donnell fans, however, is that her show will probably be around for a long, long time. By the year 2001, she will have met every living celebrity from her childhood dreams. But beneath that bubbly exterior beats the heart of a real person, not a made-for-TV creation. So O'Donnell warns her fans that someday she just might pack up her station wagon with the kids and head off to places unknown to raise her family in peace and away from the media spotlight.

And when the history of television in the twentieth century is written, her fans can be sure that Rosie O'Donnell's name will forever be mentioned in the same breath as other great talk-show hosts: Johnny Carson, Oprah Winfrey, Jay Leno, and Merv Griffin.

Notes

Chapter 1: Growing Up Roseann

1. Quoted in George Mair and Anna Green, *Rosie O'Donnell: Her True Story*. New York: Birch Lane Press, 1997, p. 4.
2. Quoted in Mair and Green, *Rosie O'Donnell: Her True Story*, p. 5.
3. Quoted in Mair and Green, *Rosie O'Donnell: Her True Story*, p. 4.
4. Quoted in Liz Smith, "Really Rosie," *Good Housekeeping*, June 1997.
5. Quoted in Smith, "Really Rosie."
6. Quoted in Mair and Green, *Rosie O'Donnell: Her True Story*, p. 5.
7. Quoted in Mair and Green, *Rosie O'Donnell: Her True Story*, p. 5.
8. Quoted in Mair and Green, *Rosie O'Donnell: Her True Story*, p. 7.
9. Quoted in Mair and Green, *Rosie O'Donnell: Her True Story*, p. 10.
10. Quoted in Patrick Pacheco, "Wondrous Rosie O'Donnell!" *Cosmopolitan*, June 1994.
11. Quoted in Melina Gerosa, "Miss Congeniality," *Ladies' Home Journal*, February 1997.
12. Kristen Golden, "Rosie O'Donnell," *Ms.*, January/February 1997.
13. Quoted in Gerosa, "Miss Congeniality."
14. Quoted in Gerosa, "Miss Congeniality."
15. Quoted in Joan Gelman, "Home Is Where Her Heart Is," *McCall's*, February 1998.
16. Quoted in Gerosa, "Miss Congeniality."
17. Quoted in Smith, "Really Rosie."
18. Quoted in Gerosa, "Miss Congeniality."
19. Quoted in Mair and Green, *Rosie O'Donnell: Her True Story*, p. 17.
20. Quoted in Mair and Green, *Rosie O'Donnell: Her True Story*, p. 18.
21. Quoted in Pacheco, "Wondrous Rosie O'Donnell!"

22. Quoted in James Robert Parish, *Rosie.* New York: Caroll & Graf, 1997, p. 35.

Chapter 2: Playing the Comedy Clubs

23. Quoted in Mair and Green, *Rosie O'Donnell: Her True Story*, p. 20.
24. Quoted in Mair and Green, *Rosie O'Donnell: Her True Story*, p. 21.
25. Quoted in Smith, "Really Rosie."
26. Quoted in Mair and Green, *Rosie O'Donnell: Her True Story*, p. 23.
27. Quoted in Mair and Green, *Rosie O'Donnell: Her True Story*, p. 24.
28. Quoted in Mair and Green, *Rosie O'Donnell: Her True Story*, p. 26.
29. Quoted in Golden, "Rosie O'Donnell."
30. Quoted in Parish, *Rosie,* p. 55.
31. Quoted in Gloria Goodman, *The Life and Humor of Rosie O'Donnell.* New York: William Morrow, 1998, pp. 24–25.
32. Quoted in Mair and Green, *Rosie O'Donnell: Her True Story*, p. 28.
33. Quoted in Goodman, *The Life and Humor of Rosie O'Donnell,* p. 27.
34. Quoted in Parish, *Rosie,* p. 49.

Chapter 3: Television Breakthrough

35. Quoted in Mair and Green, *Rosie O'Donnell: Her True Story*, p. 35.
36. Quoted in Mair and Green, *Rosie O'Donnell: Her True Story*, p. 35.
37. Quoted in Parish, *Rosie,* p. 56.
38. Quoted in Parish, *Rosie,* p. 58.
39. Quoted in Parish, *Rosie,* pp. 60–61.
40. Quoted in Goodman, *The Life and Humor of Rosie O'Donnell,* p. 51.
41. Quoted in Bruce Fretts, "Rosie O'Donnell," *Entertainment Weekly,* December 27, 1996.
42. Quoted in Goodman, *The Life and Humor of Rosie O'Donnell,* p. 53.
43. Quoted in Mair and Green, *Rosie O'Donnell: Her True Story*, p. 55.
44. Quoted in Mair and Green, *Rosie O'Donnell: Her True Story*, pp. 55–56.

Chapter 4: Rosie the Movie Star

45. Quoted in Parish, *Rosie,* p. 84.
46. Quoted in Gerosa, "Miss Congeniality."
47. Quoted in Allison Adato, "Love Ya [Kiss, Kiss] Don't Change," *Life,* July 1996.

48. Quoted in Mair and Green, *Rosie O'Donnell: Her True Story*, p. 64.
49. Quoted in Gerosa, "Miss Congeniality."
50. Quoted in Adato, "Love Ya [Kiss, Kiss] Don't Change."
51. Quoted in Adato, "Love Ya [Kiss, Kiss] Don't Change."
52. Quoted in Gerosa, "Miss Congeniality."
53. Quoted in Adato, "Love Ya [Kiss, Kiss] Don't Change."
54. Quoted in Mair and Green, *Rosie O'Donnell: Her True Story*, p. 82.
55. Quoted in Mair and Green, *Rosie O'Donnell: Her True Story*, p. 84.
56. Quoted in Mair and Green, *Rosie O'Donnell: Her True Story*, p. 90.
57. Quoted in Parish, *Rosie*, p. 146.
58. Quoted in Pacheco, "Wondrous Rosie O'Donnell!"
59. Quoted in Pacheco, "Wondrous Rosie O'Donnell!"
60. Quoted in Mair and Green, *Rosie O'Donnell: Her True Story*, p. 99.

Chapter 5: Rosie Hits the Big Time

61. Quoted in Goodman, *The Life and Humor of Rosie O'Donnell*, p. 135.
62. Quoted in Gerosa, "Miss Congeniality."
63. Quoted in Gerosa, "Miss Congeniality."
64. Quoted in Adato, "Love Ya [Kiss, Kiss] Don't Change."
65. Quoted in Smith, "Really Rosie."
66. Quoted in Martha Frankel, "Rosie's Big (and Little) New Plans," *Redbook*, October 1997.
67. Quoted in Mair and Green, *Rosie O'Donnell: Her True Story*, p. 130.
68. Quoted in Mair and Green, *Rosie O'Donnell: Her True Story*, p. 130.
69. Quoted in Smith, "Really Rosie."
70. Quoted in Rick Marin, "Coming Up Roses," *Newsweek,* July 15, 1996.
71. Quoted in Adato, "Love Ya [Kiss, Kiss] Don't Change."
72. Golden, "Rosie O'Donnell."
73. Quoted in Gerosa, "Miss Congeniality."

Chapter 6: The Real Rosie O'Donnell

74. Quoted in Mair and Green, *Rosie O'Donnell: Her True Story*, p. 246.
75. Quoted in Gerosa, "Miss Congeniality."

76. Quoted in Goodman, *The Life and Humor of Rosie O'Donnell,* p. 197.
77. Quoted in Frankel, "Rosie's Big (and Little) New Plans."
78. Quoted in Gelman, "Home Is Where Her Heart Is."
79. Quoted in Gelman, "Home Is Where Her Heart Is."
80. Quoted in Golden, "Rosie O'Donnell."
81. Quoted in Gelman, "Home Is Where Her Heart Is."
82. Quoted in Gelman, "Home Is Where Her Heart Is."
83. Quoted in Joanna Powell, "Rosie's Devotion," *Good Housekeeping,* June 1998.
84. Quoted in Powell, "Rosie's Devotion."
85. Quoted in Smith, "Really Rosie."
86. Quoted in Powell, "Rosie's Devotion."
87. Quoted in Smith, "Really Rosie."
88. Quoted in Mair and Green, *Rosie O'Donnell: Her True Story,* p. 203.
89. Quoted in Powell, "Rosie's Devotion."

Epilogue: Everything's Coming Up Rosie

90. Quoted in Cynthia Littleton, "Rosie Readies Revamp Rollout," *Variety,* August 24, 1998.
91. Quoted in Parish, *Rosie,* p. 252.

Important Dates in the Life of Rosie O'Donnell

1962—Roseann O'Donnell is born in Commack, a suburb of Long Island, New York.

1973—Her mother dies of cancer four days before her eleventh birthday.

1982—Gets her first paid job as a professional comic at Comedy Connection in Boston, Massachusetts.

1986—Makes her first appearance as a cast member of NBC television sitcom *Gimme a Break*.

1989—*Stand-up Spotlight* airs on VH1, with O'Donnell as both producer and performer.

1992—Appears in her first movie, *A League of Their Own*, and wins praise for her acting.

1995—Wins the Nickelodeon Kids' Choice Award for her role as Betty Rubble in *The Flintstones* movie, which was panned by critics but popular with kids; adopts a baby boy, Parker Jaren O'Donnell.

1996—*The Rosie O'Donnell Show* airs for the first time on nationwide television.

1997—Adopts a baby girl, Chelsea Belle O'Donnell.

1998—By January, O'Donnell's organization, For All Kids Foundation, had given out $1.5 million to 105 different children's charities.

For Further Reading

Joan Gelman, "Home Is Where Her Heart Is," *McCall's,* February 1998. An article about O'Donnell's home life, her views on child raising and other domestic issues.

Kristen Golden, "Rosie O'Donnell," *Ms.,* January/February 1997. An article in a magazine that made O'Donnell the *Ms.* magazine "Woman of the Year." This interview delves more into O'Donnell's feminist political perspective and her charity work for women and children.

Gloria Goodman, *The Life and Humor of Rosie O'Donnell.* New York: William Morrow, 1998. A touching and humorous book that chronicles Rosie O'Donnell's life, from her difficult childhood to her overwhelming popularity.

George Mair and Anna Green, *Rosie O'Donnell: Her True Story.* New York: Birch Lane Press, 1997. A book about Rosie O'Donnell's life written by George Mair, a journalist with more than thirty-six years' experience writing for CBS, the Los Angeles Times Syndicate, and HBO. Cowritten by Anna Green, a freelance editor and writer.

Patrick Pacheco, "Wondrous Rosie O'Donnell!" *Cosmopolitan,* June 1994. An earlier interview that relates O'Donnell's views on her weight, her stand-up career, and her movies.

James Robert Parish, *Rosie.* New York: Carroll & Graf, 1997. A very informative biography that contains a filmography, a list of O'Donnell's television series, and detailed explanations of the comedy club boom and glut.

Liz Smith, "Really Rosie," *Good Housekeeping,* June 1997. A very lively interview with gossip columnist Liz Smith.

Works Consulted

Allison Adato, "Love Ya [Kiss, Kiss] Don't Change," *Life*, July 1996. An article in which O'Donnell is quoted on the making of *A League of Their Own* and other movies.

Martha Frankel, "Rosie's Big (and Little) New Plans," *Redbook*, October 1997. An article about O'Donnell's children, the adoption process, and her methods of child care.

Bruce Fretts, "Rosie O'Donnell," *Entertainment Weekly*, December 27, 1996. An article that discussses O'Donnell's movies and her views on the entertainment business.

Melina Gerosa, "Miss Congeniality," *Ladies' Home Journal*, February 1997. A general article about the life and career of Rosie.

Cynthia Littleton, "Rosie Readies Revamp Rollout," *Variety*, August 24, 1998. This article, written for the show-business magazine *Variety*, discusses the business side of O'Donnell's talk show as it began its third season on the air.

Rick Marin, "Coming Up Roses," *Newsweek*, July 15, 1996. An article about sleaze on daytime TV and how O'Donnell is a refreshing answer to the Springers and other trash-talk show hosts.

Rosie O'Donnell, ed., *Kids Are Punny: Jokes Sent by Kids to The Rosie O'Donnell Show*. New York: Warner Books, 1997. A book full of jokes sent to Rosie O'Donnell by children.

———, *Kids Are Punny 2: Jokes Sent by Kids to The Rosie O'Donnell Show*. New York: Warner Books, 1998. A second book of kids' jokes edited by O'Donnell.

Joanna Powell, "Rosie's Devotion," *Good Housekeeping*, June 1998. An article about O'Donnell's commitment to women and children.

Rosie O'Donnell On-Line

Official Site of *The Rosie O'Donnell Show*

Features such segments as show info, "Cutie Patootie Parenting Tips," how to contact O'Donnell for tickets, and a scrapbook of the show's best moments.

http://www.rosieo.warnerbros.com/

The ACME Rosie Page

A full-service Rosie O'Donnell fan page that puts the web surfer onto the "web ring" with more than half a dozen O'Donnell fan pages.

http://www.bestware.net/spreng/rosie/index.html

Index

Picture Credits

Cover photo: Archive Photos/Darlene Hammond
A. Ortega/Sipa Press, 63, 78
AP Photo/Bill Kostroun, 72
AP Photo/Nick Ut, 83
Archive Photos, 14
© David Allen/Corbis, 74
Corbis-Bettmann, 47
Darlene Hammond/Archive Photos, 80
Fred Prouser/Sipa Press, 59, 73
Lee/Archive Newsphotos, 62
Marcel Thomas/Sipa Press, 56
Photofest, 9, 17, 19, 21, 25, 27, 32, 37, 44, 48, 52, 54, 57, 64, 70
Reuters/Fred Prouser/Archive Photos, 36
Reuters/Sam Mircovich/Archive Photos, 50
UPI/Corbis-Bettmann, 13

About the Author

Stuart A. Kallen is the author of more than 135 nonfiction books for children and young adults. He has written on topics ranging from the theory of relativity to rock-and-roll history to life on the American frontier. In addition, Mr. Kallen has written award-winning children's videos and television scripts. Mr. Kallen lives in San Diego, California.

NORTH SMITHFIELD PUBLIC LIBRARY

8 5944 00060 9014

APR xx'00 DATE DUE

APR 0 3 2001	

BRODART, CO.   Cat. No. 23-221-003